“How Woul
Pretend?”

“Shouldn’t take more than a month.”

“A month as your fiancée.”

“Yeah.”

“No touching of any kind. No kissing—”

“Hold on.” David stopped her in midstream. “We have to convince this guy we’re a real couple. So there *will* be touching. And kissing. And there will be you looking at me with adoration.”

She laughed.

He frowned.

“Fine, fine,” she said, waving a hand at him. “I’ll be a good fiancée and the occasional touch or kiss—in public—is okay.”

“Then we have a deal.” He held out one hand to her and waited for her to take it.

Nodding, Mia slid her hand into his and couldn’t help feeling that just maybe she was swimming in waters *way* too deep for her.

The Lone Star Cinderella

MAUREEN CHILD

All the characters in this book have no existence outside the imagination of the author, and have no relation whatsoever to anyone bearing the same name or names. They are not even distantly inspired by any individual known or unknown to the author, and all the incidents are pure invention.

First published in Great Britain 2013
by Mills & Boon, an imprint of Harlequin (UK) Limited,
Large Print edition 2013
Harlequin (UK) Limited,
Eton House, 18-24 Paradise Road,
Richmond, Surrey TW9 1SR

Special thanks and acknowledgment to Maureen Child for her contribution to *Texas Cattleman's Club: The Missing Mogul* miniseries.

ISBN: 978 0 263 23801 3

Harlequin (UK) policy is to use papers that are natural, renewable and recyclable products and made from wood grown in sustainable forests. The logging and manufacturing process conform to the legal environmental regulations of the country of origin.

Printed and bound in Great Britain
by CPI Antony Rowe, Chippenham, Wiltshire

MAUREEN CHILD

writes for Mills & Boon® Desire and can't imagine a better job. Being able to indulge your love for romance as well as being able to spin stories just the way you want them told is, in a word, perfect.

A seven-time finalist for the prestigious Romance Writers of America RITA® Award, Maureen is the author of more than one hundred romance novels. Her books regularly appear on the bestseller lists and have won several awards, including the Prism, the National Readers' Choice Award, the Colorado Romance Writers Award of Excellence and the Golden Quill.

One of her books, *The Soul Collector*, was made into a CBS TV movie starring Melissa Gilbert, Bruce Greenwood and Ossie Davis. If you look closely, in the last five minutes of the movie, you'll spot Maureen, who was an extra in the last scene.

Maureen believes that laughter goes hand in hand with love, so her stories are always filled with humour. The many letters she receives assures her that her readers love to laugh as much as she does.

Maureen Child is a native Californian, but has recently moved to the mountains of Utah. She loves a new adventure, though the thought of having to deal with snow for the first time is a little intimidating.

To Kate Carlisle and Jennifer Apodaca—
great friends and wonderful writers
who helped keep me sane during
the writing of this book!

One

Dave Firestone was a man on a mission.

The future of his ranch was at stake and damned if he was going to let scandal or whispered rumors ruin what he'd spent years building. It had been months now since Alex Santiago had disappeared and Dave *still* felt a cloud of suspicion hanging around his head. Time to find out one way or the other what the law in town thought of the situation.

He climbed out of his 4x4, tugged the collar of his brown leather jacket up around his neck and squinted into the East Texas wind. October was rolling in cold, signaling what would be an even colder winter. Nothing he could do about that, but Dave had driven to the border of his ranch to get at least one part of his life straightened out.

A tall man wearing a worn, black leather coat and a tan, wide-brimmed hat was patching the barbed-wire fence that separated Dave's ranch, the Royal Round Up, from the neighboring ranch, the Battlelands. Behind the man in black, another man, Bill Hardesty, a Battle ranch hand, unloaded wire from a battered truck. Dave nodded a greeting to Bill, then focused his attention on Nathan Battle.

Nathan looked up as Dave approached. "Hey, Dave, how's it going?"

"Going fine," he said, because Dave Firestone never admitted to having a problem he couldn't solve. "I went by the main ranch house and Jake told me where I could find you. Didn't think I'd find the town sheriff out fixing fence line."

Nathan shrugged and glanced out over the surrounding land before shifting his gaze back to Dave. "I like getting out on the ranch. Gives me a chance to think. Clear my head. My brother does most of the heavy lifting on the Battlelands, but I'm a full partner and it feels good to get back to basics, you know?" Then he grinned. "Besides, Amanda's on a remodeling binge, getting ready for the baby. So we've got one of Sam Gordon's construction crews at the house all the time. Being out here..." he said, then sighed in pleasure. "Quiet."

From his spot on the truck, Bill snorted. "Enjoy it while it lasts, boss. Once that baby comes you can kiss 'quiet' goodbye forever."

Nathan chuckled, then said, "Just unload the wire, will ya?"

Dave ignored the byplay. He wished he'd found Nathan alone out here, but he was going to have his say whether Bill was listening in or not.

Things had changed a lot around Royal in the past few months, Dave thought. Nathan and Amanda were married and expecting a baby. Sam and Lila were expecting twins. And then there was the reason Dave had come to see Nathan on his day off.

The disappearance of Alex Santiago.

He wouldn't claim to have been friends with Alex, but he'd never wished the man harm, either. This vanishing act of his was weird enough to keep the people in town talking—and most of them were talking about how Dave and Alex had been business rivals and wondering if maybe Alex hadn't had some help in disappearing.

Dave had never been one to give a flying damn what people had to say about him. He ran his life and his business the way he saw fit, and if people didn't like it, screw them. But like he'd just been thinking, things had changed. Irritating to admit that gossip and the threat of scandal had chased him out here to talk to the town sheriff, but there it was.

"Yeah, I get that. My foreman's the best there is, but I like doing ranch work on my own, too. Always have," Dave said, snatching his hat off to stab his fingers through his hair. "And I hate to ruin your peace and quiet…"

Nathan hooked his pair of wire cutters into the tool belt at his waist and looked at Dave. "But?"

"But," Dave said, with the briefest of glances toward Bill, who wasn't even bothering to hide his interest in the conversation, "I need to know

if you've got anything new on Alex's disappearance."

Scowling, Nathan admitted, "I've got nothing. It's like he dropped off the face of the earth. No action on his credit or debit cards, either. Haven't got a clue what happened to him and, to tell you the truth, it's making me nuts."

"I can imagine," Dave said and tipped the brim of his hat back a bit. "It's not doing much for me, either."

Nathan nodded grimly. "Yeah, I've heard the whispers."

"Great." Just what he wanted. The town sheriff listening to rumors about him.

"Relax." Nathan waved one hand at him and shook his head. "I know what the gossips in this town are like, Dave. Hell, they almost cost me Amanda." He paused for a second as if considering what might have been. Then he shook his head again and said, "If it helps any, you're officially *not* a suspect."

He hadn't really thought he was, but it was good to hear anyway. It didn't solve his problem, but knowing that Nathan believed in his innocence was one less thing to worry about. Dave knew how it must have looked to everyone in town. He was among the last people to have seen Alex before he went missing. And the argument they'd had on Main Street had been witnessed by at least a dozen people.

Plus, it was pretty much common knowledge around Royal that Alex had snapped up the investment property that Dave had had his eye on. So yeah, Dave had been furious. But he hadn't wanted anything to happen to Alex.

"Glad to hear you say that," Dave finally said. "In fact, it's what I came out here to ask you. Feels good knowing I'm not a suspect, I'll admit. But it doesn't change how people in this town are looking at me."

He'd been in Royal three years, and he would have thought people would know him by now. But apparently, one whisper of juicy gossip was all it took to have people looking at him with a jaundiced eye.

Nathan dropped one hand to the top of the fence post and said, "People talk, you can't stop it. God knows I've tried. And in a town the size of Royal, that's about all they've got to do to fill the time, you know? Doesn't mean anything."

"Not to you, maybe—and I'm grateful, don't get me wrong," Dave told him. "But I'm trying to land a contract with TexCat and—"

Nathan chuckled and stopped him. "No need to say more. Hell, Texas Cattle is legendary. Everyone in the state knows about Thomas Buckley and how he runs his company. The old man is such a straight arrow…" He broke off. "That's why the concern over the gossip."

"Yeah, if Buckley hears those rumors, I'll never get the contract with him to sell my beef." Scandal could sour the deal before it was made, and damned if Dave would let that happen.

TexCat was the biggest beef buyer in the country. But it was a family-run company and Buckley himself ran it along the narrowest lines possible. No scandal had ever touched his company, and he was determined to keep it that way. So if he got wind of rumors about Dave now, it would only make all of this more difficult.

"Ol' Buckley is so worried about what people think," Bill pointed out from his spot on the truck, "I hear he *sleeps* in a three-piece suit."

Dave frowned and Nathan shot Bill a look. "Is that wire unloaded?"

"Almost," Bill said and ducked his head as he went back to work.

"Sorry," Nathan said unnecessarily, then grinned. "Everybody's got something to say about everything around here. But you already know that, don't you?"

"You could say so," Dave muttered.

Still smiling, Nathan added, "Where Buckley's concerned, it's not just the rumors you've got to be worried about."

Dave frowned. "Yeah, I know."

Nathan's smile widened. "Buckley only deals with married family men. Last time I looked, you were single. I figure the rumors and whispering should be the least of your problems. How're you planning on coming up with a wife?"

Dave huffed out a disgusted breath. "Haven't figured that part out yet. We're just at the beginning of negotiations with TexCat. I've still got some time." He jammed his hat back on his head and hunched deeper into his jacket as a sharp, cold wind slapped at them. "I'll think of something."

Nathan nodded. "If not, TexCat isn't the only beef buyer in the world."

"No," Dave agreed. "But they're the best."

He wanted that contract. And what Dave Firestone wanted, he got. Period. He'd clawed and fought and earned his success the hard way. Not a chance in hell he'd stop before he was finished.

Mia Hughes opened the pantry door and stared inside at the nearly empty shelves as if expecting more food to suddenly appear. Naturally, that didn't happen. So, with a sigh, she grabbed another package of Top Ramen and headed for the stove.

"Honestly, if I have to eat noodles much longer…" She filled a pan with a cup of water, turned on the fire underneath and watched it, waiting for it to boil. She glanced at the package in her hand. "At least this one is beef flavor. Maybe if I close my eyes while I eat it I can pretend it's a burger."

Well, that image made her stomach growl. She

slapped one hand to her belly as if to appease it somehow. It didn't work. She was on the ragged edge and had been for a few weeks now.

As Alex Santiago's housekeeper, she'd had access to the household account at the bank. But she'd been using that money to pay utility bills and the hundreds of other things that had come up since Alex had disappeared. She hadn't had any extra to waste on trivial things like her salary or *food.* So she'd made do with the staples that had been in the pantry and freezer. But the cupboards were practically bare now and only ice cubes were left in the freezer. And it wasn't as if she had money coming in. Even her intern position at Royal Junior High was ending soon. She couldn't go out and get a job, either. What if Alex called the house while she was gone?

"Of course," she reassured herself aloud, "the upside is you've lost five pounds in the past couple of weeks. Downside? I'm ready to chew on a table leg."

Her voice echoed in the cavernous kitchen. The room was spotless, but that was due more to the fact that it hadn't seen much action in the past few months than to Mia's cleaning abilities. Though she took her duties as housekeeper seriously and kept the palatial mansion sparkling throughout. Still, since Alex went missing a few months ago, there hadn't been much for Mia to do in the big house.

The water came to a boil and she stirred in the dried noodles and flavor packet before putting the lid on the pan again then moving it off the heat to steep. While she waited for her lunch, she wandered to the wide windows overlooking the stone patio and the backyard beyond.

From this vantage point, she could also see the rooflines of Alex's neighbors, though the homes in the luxurious subdivision known as Pine Valley weren't crowded together. Each home was different, custom designed and built by the owners, and each sat on a wide, wooded lot so there was plenty of privacy.

Right now though, Mia had too much privacy. She'd been alone in the house since Alex's disappearance. Alone with a phone that hadn't stopped ringing in weeks. Reporters hounded her anytime she left the house, so she rarely left anymore.

Since Pine Valley was a gated community, only a few reporters had managed to sneak past the gate guard to annoy her. But she knew that wouldn't last. The longer Alex was gone, the more brazen reporters would become.

A wealthy man going missing was big news. Especially in a town the size of Royal.

She tapped her short, neat fingernails against the cold, smooth, black granite countertop. Mia's stomach did a slow turn and she swallowed hard. Alex had been good to her. He'd given her a job when she'd most needed one. He'd allowed her the space to continue her education and because of that, she was close to getting her counseling degree.

Not only did Mia really owe Alex, she liked him, too. He'd become a good friend as well as her employer, and Mia didn't have many friends. She stared blankly out the window and absently noted the treetops whipping in the cold October wind. She shivered involuntarily and turned her back on the view. She didn't want to think about winter coming and Alex still being gone. She hated not knowing if her friend was safe. Or hurt. But she had to keep positive and believe that Alex would come home.

She also couldn't help worrying about what she was going to do next. The bills had been paid, true. But her tuition was due soon and if Alex wasn't there to pay her…

When the phone rang, she jumped and instinctively reached for it before stopping herself and letting it go to the answering machine. Weeks ago, she'd decided to let the machine pick up so she could screen her calls, in an attempt to avoid reporters and the unceasing questions she couldn't answer.

Still, she was always hoping that somehow the caller might be Alex, telling her he was fine, and sorry he'd worried her and oh, that he was wiring more money into the household accounts. Not very realistic, but Mia's innate optimism was hard to discourage.

The machine kicked on and after the beep, a female voice asked, "Mia? You there? If you're listening, pick up."

Smiling, she snatched up the receiver. "Sophie, hi."

"Still dodging reporters?"

"Every day," she said and leaned back against the counter. Her gaze slid to the backyard again and the trees waving and dancing in the wind. "They don't give up."

"At least they can't get past the gate guard there to bother you in person."

"A few of them have managed, but one call to security and that's taken care of." Though she hated feeling as though she was living through a medieval siege. And she had to admit that living alone in this big house made her a little nervous at night. Yes, Royal was a safe place, and a gated community should have made her feel even more secure. But with Alex gone and the world wondering *why,* Mia was always worried that someone might come sneaking around the house at night, looking for clues or a story. But Mia didn't want her thoughts to go to the dark side. Alex was missing, yes. But she couldn't allow herself to think he was gone forever.

"My offer to come and stay with me for a while still holds, you know."

Sophie Beldon was a good friend. She was also Alex's assistant, and since his disappearance, the two women had become even closer friends. Together, they'd done all they could to search for Alex, and still had come up empty. But they had another plan now. One that had Mia looking for more information on Dave Firestone, a business rival of Alex's. Of course, she hadn't actually *started* on that plan yet, since she had no idea how to go about it.

"Really, thank you. It's tempting, believe me," Mia confessed. But she couldn't very well move in with her friend and leave Alex's house unguarded. Not to mention that Mia hated the idea of mooching meals from Sophie. She didn't like asking people for anything. She was far too used to doing things herself and she didn't see that changing anytime soon. "It's really nice of you to offer, Sophie. But I really want to be here. In case Alex calls or comes back. Besides, I wouldn't feel right leaving his house vacant."

"Okay. I can understand all of that," Sophie said. "But if you change your mind, the offer stands. So how's everything else going? Is there anything I can do?"

"No, but thanks." Mia cringed a little, hating

that her friend knew just how bad off Mia was. The two of them had gone out to lunch just a couple weeks ago and when she'd tried to pay the bill, as a thank-you to Sophie for being so nice, Mia's debit card had been denied. Her bank account hadn't had enough in it to pay for a simple *lunch.* Mortified, Mia had been forced to let Sophie pay for their meals.

She hated this. Hated worrying about money. Hated worrying about Alex. She just wanted her nice, safe, comfortable life back. Was that really so much to ask?

"We're friends, Mia." Sophie's voice was soft and low. "I know you need money. Why won't you let me help you out temporarily? It would just be a loan. When Alex comes home, you can pay me back."

Again, so very tempting. But she didn't know how or when she could pay her friend back, so she couldn't accept the loan. Mia Hughes paid her own way. Always. Heck, she didn't even have a credit card because she paid cash or she didn't buy.

"Sophie," she said on a sigh, "I *really* appreciate the offer. But we've been looking for Alex for months and it's like he vanished off the face of the earth. We don't know when he'll come back." *If ever,* her mind added, but she didn't say it aloud, not wanting to tempt whatever gods might be listening in on them. "I'm fine. Honest. The thing with my debit card was just a bank mistake." Okay, a small lie, but one she would cling to. She didn't want her friend worried about her and she simply could not accept a loan. Mia had been making her own way in the world since she was eighteen, and she wouldn't start looking for handouts now. No matter how hungry she was.

"You have the hardest head," Sophie murmured.

Mia smiled. "Thank you."

"Wasn't a compliment," her friend assured her on a laugh. "But okay. I'll let it go. For *now.*"

"I appreciate it."

"That's not why I called, anyway," Sophie said.

Instantly, Mia's friend radar started humming. Sophie had only recently become engaged to Zach Lassiter, Alex's business partner. After a shaky start, the two were so happy together, Mia was afraid that something had gone wrong between them. "Are you and Zach okay?"

"We're fine. He's great. This isn't about us."

"Okay, then," Mia said as she carried the phone across the kitchen, lifted the lid on her lunch and sighed before setting the lid back in place. "What is it about?"

"Remember how we talked about you going out to gather more information on Dave Firestone?"

"Yeah," Mia said. "I don't have anything yet, though. I'm not exactly a private investigator." She'd tried internet searches, but so far all she had found were the sanitized information blurbs you found about *any* wealthy, successful man. And she wasn't sure where to dig up anything else.

"Well," Sophie told her, "I have something. I just got off the phone with Carrie Hardesty."

Mia frowned, trying to place the name. Before she could say she didn't know the woman, Sophie was continuing.

"Carrie's husband, Bill, is a ranch hand on the Battlelands."

"Uh-huh." She still didn't see what this had to do with her or Dave Firestone or why she might be interested. And now she was hungry enough that she was even anxious for her beef-flavored noodle lunch.

"So Bill called Carrie to tell her he'd be home early today because he and Nathan had finished work faster than they'd thought despite an interruption."

"Okay..." Mia had to smile. She still had no idea why this should interest her, but Sophie's voice had taken on that storytelling tone, so she didn't stop her.

"Bill told Carrie that Dave Firestone had shown up to talk to Nathan."

Mia stiffened. Dave had been one of the last people to see her employer before he disappeared. She'd heard the talk around town. She knew that people were wondering if Dave had had something to do with Alex going missing. But she also knew that gossip was the fuel that kept small towns going, so she didn't really put a lot of stock in it.

Still, though, Dave Firestone was wealthy, determined and too gorgeous to be trusted. Plus, she and Sophie had decided to check the man out.

"What was he talking to Nathan about?"

"Apparently, he went there to find out if he was a suspect in Alex's disappearance."

Mia sucked in a gulp of air. "He did?"

"Yep," Sophie said, then added, "but Bill says Nathan assured Dave that he was officially *not* a suspect."

Disappointment curled in the pit of her stomach. Not that she wished Dave Firestone arrested or anything, but she wanted answers. Soon.

"It's not surprising," Mia said, chewing at her bottom lip. "Dave Firestone is an important man around here. There would have to be *serious* evidence against him for Nathan to keep him as a suspect."

"I know." Sophie sounded as dejected as Mia felt.

"Tell the truth, Soph," Mia said. "Do you really think Dave is involved in Alex's disappearance?"

"Probably not." Her friend sighed.

"Me, either," Mia agreed.

"But he's the only link we have, Mia. I think

we should stick to our plan and you should find out anything you can about him. Even if Dave is innocent, he might still know something that he doesn't even know he knows, you know?"

Mia laughed a little. "Sadly, I understood that completely."

Sophie added, "And according to what Bill told Carrie, Nathan admitted that he doesn't have a clue what happened to Alex."

Her heart sank a little further at that news. Of course, she'd thought as much. Nathan Battle had been working this case for months and he'd kept her apprised of his lack of progress. The sheriff and Alex were good friends, so Mia knew that Nathan was just as much personally involved in the search as he was professionally.

And none of that had helped them find Alex.

In the time Mia had worked for Alex Santiago, she'd known him to be warm, generous and kind. But he also had secrets. No one was allowed in his home office, for example. He had only allowed Mia in to clean once a month and then only if he was present. And when she and Sophie had started comparing notes, Sophie had told her about the secret phone calls Alex had been getting.

Since Alex had been gone, Mia had searched his home office top to bottom and Sophie had gone through his emails and phone records, but they hadn't discovered a thing.

Which told her that either Alex had taken whatever he'd been safeguarding with him—or whoever had taken Alex had also gone through that office and taken what they'd found.

There was that now familiar twist of worry inside. Where was Alex? Was he hurt? Was he…

"He'll show up," Mia said, cutting short a disturbing train of thought. "There's a reasonable explanation for all of this and when Alex comes back, it will all make sense."

"You really believe that, don't you?"

"Absolutely." *Almost,* she added silently. But Mia had spent so much of her life searching for the silver lining in dark skies that it was instinctive now. She wouldn't give up on Alex and, until he was home, she would do whatever she could to help find him.

Even if it meant eating enough flavored noodles to sink a battleship.

"Oops," Sophie said suddenly, "Zach's at the door. He's taking me to lunch at the diner. I'll talk to you later, okay?"

Mia said goodbye, wishing she were at the diner right now, too. What she wouldn't give for a hamburger, fries and a shake. Sighing, she let the wish go and dumped her noodles into a bowl. Grabbing a fork, she took a bite and tried to swallow her disappointment along with the noodles.

A knock sounded at the front door and Mia took it as a reprieve from her boring lunch. She set the bowl down on the counter and headed through the house. Whoever it was knocked again, faster and louder this time, and she frowned. Did another reporter get past the gate?

At the doorway, she glanced through the glass panes on one side of the heavy door and gaped at the man standing on the porch. Before she could think about it, she yanked the door open and faced Dave Firestone.

He wore black jeans, a dark red collared shirt, a battered brown bomber jacket and scarred boots.

He held his hat in one fist, and his dark blond hair ruffled in the wind. His gray eyes locked onto her and Mia felt a jolt of something unexpected sizzle inside her.

"Mia," he said, his voice deep enough to rumble along her spine, "I think we should talk."

Two

"What're you doing here?"

Dave took a good long look at the woman standing there glaring at him. Her long, dark brown hair was, as usual, pulled back from her face and twisted into a messy knot at the back of her neck. She wore faded blue jeans and a long-sleeved, navy blue T-shirt. Her feet were bare and he was surprised to see her toes were painted fire-engine red. Mia Hughes had never seemed like the red nail polish type to him. She was more of a pastel woman, seemingly determined to fade into the background. Or so he'd thought.

Something inside him stirred whether he'd

wanted it to or not. He lifted his gaze to hers and the strength of her even stare punched out at him. Her wide blue eyes were unenhanced, yet they still seemed to captivate him.

He didn't want to be captivated.

"I think we should talk. About Alex."

"How did you get in here? The gate guard should have called me."

"I asked him not to." He shrugged. "He knows me, so it wasn't a problem."

"Well, it should have been. He never should have let you in here without contacting me." She folded her arms across her chest.

Dave scowled. He wasn't used to being kept cooling his heels outside. But Mia Hughes was guarding Alex Santiago's front door like a trained pit bull. "I think it'd be better if we went inside to talk."

"First, tell me what this is about." She cocked her head and the toes of one foot began to tap impatiently.

"I'm not your enemy." He took a step closer and noticed that she didn't move back but held her ground. He could admire that even as she frustrated him.

He'd come here to compare notes. To see if she knew anything that might shed a light on Alex's disappearance. But damned if he was going to have this conversation on the porch.

"No," she conceded. "You're not." Her stance relaxed just a fraction. "And I was going to call you later anyway…"

"Is that right?" Surprised, he took another slow look at her and he noted that her eyes were gleaming with something he could only call interest. "About what?"

"About Alex, of course," she told him with a shake of her head.

"Well, it's good that I showed up today, isn't it? Because that's just what I want to talk to you about." He glanced over his shoulder at the empty, meticulously kept grounds before looking back at her. "I want to know if there's anything you know about Alex that you haven't told Nathan Battle."

"Of course there isn't," she said, clearly insulted. "Do you really think I haven't been helping the police? I've done everything I can think of to find Alex."

"That's not what I meant," he said, cutting her off before she could erupt into a full-on rant. Hell, Mia Hughes was usually so quiet he hardly noticed her. But apparently on her own turf she wasn't so reticent.

"It better not be," she countered, and those blue eyes of hers flashed dangerously.

"Look, you don't have to be so defensive. Alex and I weren't exactly friends..."

She laughed shortly.

He frowned and continued, "But that doesn't mean I wish him harm. Hell, right now I want to find him more than anybody in this town."

A second or two passed in tense silence before she sighed and her stance relaxed. "Okay, I can understand that."

"Thanks," he muttered. "So can I come in and talk to you about this now?"

"I guess—" She stopped, looked over his shoulder at the yard and said, "Don't!"

Instantly on alert, Dave whirled around and saw a young man, somewhere in his early twenties, aiming a digital camera at them and clicking away.

"Hey," Dave said, stepping off the porch toward the man.

The guy jumped backward, shaking his head and grinning. He held out a digital recorder and shouted, "Great pictures! Chester Devon from All The News blog. Care to comment?"

"The only comment I have is one you can't print, Chester," Dave told him as he stalked toward the reporter, who had somehow slipped past the Pine Valley gate guard. "And no pictures, either."

"Free country, man," Chester countered, still grinning. "I think my readers will be interested to see Santiago's housekeeper and a suspect in his disappearance looking so cozy…"

His readers, Dave thought. All ten of 'em. Still, if this guy posted pictures to his blog, they would eventually get around and make for more of the kind of scandal he was trying to avoid.

"Cozy? Oh, for—" Mia broke off, then spoke up again, louder. "I'm calling security."

Just what he needed, Dave thought grimly. Not

only a reporter but security coming over, too. More food for the local gossips. He couldn't do anything about Mia's call to security, but maybe he could head the reporter off at the pass.

"I'll give you a thousand dollars for your camera."

"Are you serious?" the kid asked with a laugh. "No way, man."

Great. A budding reporter with morals. Or maybe Dave just hadn't hit the guy's price yet. "Five thousand."

Chester wavered.

Dave could see it in the kid's eyes. He was thinking that with five grand in his pocket he could buy a better camera, maybe get a job at a real newspaper.

"I don't know..." Chester ran one hand across the chin sprouting a few stray whiskers. "With this kind of shot, I could maybe get a job at a paper in Houston."

Dave understood the kid's dreams. He'd had a hell of a lot of them himself once. And he'd worked his ass off to make sure they all came true. Didn't mean he was going to be the rung on the ladder beneath Chester's feet, though.

"Haven't you heard, kid? Newspapers are dinosaurs."

"True..."

Dave had the kid now. This guy wasn't enough of a poker player to hide the avarice in his eyes. Everyone had his price, Dave reminded himself. All he had to do was find the right number and this guy would cave. "Call it ten thousand and I want your recorder, too."

"Seriously?" Chester's eyes lit up. "You got a deal, man."

The kid followed while Dave went to his car, grabbed a checkbook from the glove compartment and wrote out a check. He signed it, then held one hand out.

"Let's have 'em," Dave said. The kid laid his camera and the recorder on Dave's palm, then snatched the check. He stared at it for a couple seconds, a slow smile spreading on his face.

"This is seriously cool, man. With this, I can get out of Royal and move to Houston."

"Good." The farther away the better, as far as

Dave was concerned. "You should get moving before security gets here and starts asking you uncomfortable questions."

The kid looked up and grinned. "I'm practically gone."

A second later, Chester was sprinting off across the yard, and then lost in the scrub oaks and pines defining the edge of Alex's lot. Probably scaled the fence to get in here, Dave thought and had to give the kid points. He approved of determination. He also approved of getting rid of the kid as easily as possible.

Ten thousand was nothing. He'd have paid twice that to keep Chester quiet. As that thought moved through his mind, Dave realized that his problem might not be completely solved. Just because Chester didn't have photographic proof didn't mean he'd be quiet about Dave's visit to Mia.

So it was time to put a different spin on this. His mind raced with possible solutions and almost instantly, he came up with a workable plan. And if he worked it right, this could actually solve all of his problems. He glanced toward the house, where Mia was again standing in the open front doorway.

A Pine Valley security car pulled up to the curb and a uniformed guard stepped out. Before he could speak, Dave pointed and called out, "He ran toward the ravine."

The security guard hopped back into his car and went in pursuit, but Dave knew that kid was going to evade the guard. He'd gotten *in* to the gated community without being caught, hadn't he?

"What's going on?" Mia stepped out onto the wide, brick porch. "How'd you get him to leave?"

"Made him an offer," Dave said as he walked toward her.

She blinked at him. "You paid him off?"

"I did." Dave took the porch steps and stood directly opposite her. "Bought his camera and recorder."

She looked up at him and he could see disdain in her eyes. "It's easy for you, isn't it? Just buy people if you have to."

"I didn't buy *him,*" Dave corrected with a smile. "I bought his stuff."

"And his silence," she added.

"In theory," Dave agreed. "But there's nothing to stop him from spreading this around, despite his lack of evidence."

She wrapped her arms around her middle. "Then paying him off accomplished nothing?"

"It bought me some time," he said, mind still racing.

"Time for what?"

"That's something we should talk about." The more he considered his idea, the better he liked it.

When Alex had disappeared, Dave had hired an investigator. He'd seen the writing on the wall and had known that sooner or later, people would start suspecting *him.* As always, he'd figured it was better to be prepared. The investigator hadn't turned up much information on Alex, but Dave now knew enough about Mia to convince him he could get her to go along with his plan.

"But first," he said, meeting her eyes, "tell me. Do you think I should be a suspect?"

She looked at him for a long, silent minute. He knew she was thinking that over and it irritated him more than a little that it was taking her so long to make a judgment call. “Well?”

She slumped one shoulder against the doorjamb. “Probably not.”

His mouth quirked. “A resounding testimonial.”

“I don’t know you well enough for that.”

“Right. Well. That’s something else we should talk about.” He glanced over his shoulder at the empty yard and scanned the tree line looking for another sneaky reporter. He’d learned over the years that reporters were like ants at a picnic. First you saw one. Then two. Then the picnic was over.

“Can I come in?”

“All right.” She stepped back, allowing him to pass by. Dave caught the faintest whiff of a light, floral scent that reminded him of summer.

Once in the house, Dave headed for the living room. He’d been here before, to meet with Alex. It was a nice house. Plush but tasteful. Cream-colored walls, bold, dark red-leather sofas and chairs and heavy dark tables. The windows looked out across the yard and were tinted, making it easy to see out but almost impossible to see in.

"What's this about?" Mia asked.

Dave turned to look at her. "I'll come right to the point. Alex being missing is hard on both of us."

"Is that right?" she asked. "How are you suffering?"

"Gossip." He tossed his hat onto the nearest couch, then shoved both hands into his jeans pockets. "The whispers and rumors about me might screw up a deal I'm working on."

"A deal?" Her eyes widened. "Alex is missing and you're worried about a deal?"

"Life goes on." He said it flatly. Cold and hard. He saw reaction glitter in her eyes and he could appreciate that. He admired loyalty. "I didn't have anything to do with Alex's disappearance and I don't think you did, either."

She laughed shortly. "Well, thanks very much. I didn't know I was a suspect."

"Why wouldn't you be? You're his housekeeper."

"You can't be serious."

"Why not?"

The look on her face was pure astonishment.

And no, he wasn't serious. No one would ever suspect Mia Hughes of anything illegal. She was quiet, shy—or at least she had always seemed so until this morning—and she didn't exactly come off as a femme fatale. First, she was too skittish to be involved in any kind of plot. She'd blow the whole thing in minutes if it came down to it. And secondly, she was just too all-American-girl-next-door.

Shiny red toenails notwithstanding.

But throwing her off balance was just what Dave needed. Because he needed her. In fact, she was damn near perfect. The plan that had occurred to him while he was dealing with the would-be reporter actually depended on her. If she agreed—and she *would*—then he had a way to explain him being here—should the kid decide to go ahead and post to his blog anyway. And it might also appease Thomas Buckley and his narrow view of life. What Dave needed was a wife. Not a real wife, mind you. But something temporary. Something that would buy him the time he needed to clinch the deal he wanted. But the women he normally went out with would never convince Thomas Buckley they were the home-and-hearth type.

Mia Hughes, on the other hand, was just the woman for the job.

"I've got a proposition for you."

"And why should I listen?"

"Because it benefits both of us," he said simply. "And you're too smart to say no before you've heard me out."

Her lips pressed together and her eyes narrowed. "Flattery?"

"Truth."

She took a breath and blew it out again in a huff. "Okay, I'm listening."

He rubbed one hand across his face, then waved at the big red-leather sofa. "Have a seat."

Obviously still on guard, she walked to the couch and perched on the edge, clearly ready to bolt the moment he said the wrong thing. Well, Dave wasn't about to blow this. He had never once gone into a negotiation blind and today was no different. Didn't matter that he hadn't come here with this plan in mind. He was flexible enough that he could turn any situation around to his favor.

Dave stood in front of the couch, looking down at Mia. “I need a wife.”

“*Excuse* me?” She started to rise but he waved her back down.

“Relax,” he said. “I’m talking more of a fantasy wife than the real thing.”

Fantasy? It was laughable, really. In what parallel universe would Mia Hughes be *anyone’s,* let alone Dave Firestone’s, fantasy? This was either some bizarre joke or he really was nuts.

“Relax?” Mia jumped to her feet, unable to sit still a moment longer. She and Sophie had wanted to check Dave out, which was the main reason Mia had allowed him into the house in the first place. But if she’d known what he was going to say she’d have left him on the porch and thrown the deadbolt to keep him out. “I really think you should go.”

He shook his head and stood his ground. He was so tall that even with Mia on her feet, he was looking down at her.

"Not until you've heard me out."

"Oh, I think I've heard enough," Mia assured him. She tried to move past him to lead him to the door, but he laid one hand on her arm and stopped her.

She felt the burn of his hand on her skin and told herself to get over it. To pay no attention. But inside, her hormones were concentrating on that rush of heat. This was so not good. He was too tall. Too gorgeous. Too sure of himself.

He smiled as if he knew what she was thinking, feeling. Well, she'd wanted to know more about Dave Firestone. Now she knew just how formidable he was. And she was worried he was just a little crazy.

His hand fell from her arm and, despite her best intentions, Mia missed that blast of heat from his fingertips. Okay, maybe he wasn't nuts. But he was…distracting.

Then he was talking again. "I'm working on a deal with Texas Cattle—the best company in the state for beef buying—but the head of the company is a pretty conservative guy. He only deals with family men. Thinks they're more stable or something. Anyway, the upshot is, I need a temporary wife—or at the very least a fiancée. Just long enough for me to seal this deal. Once that's done, we'll 'break up' and it's over."

"You're crazy."

"Just determined," he assured her. "I know money's got to be tight with Alex gone."

She stiffened and lifted her chin.

"With him wherever the hell he is, you're not being paid and," he paused to let that sink in, then added, "the household account you have access to is almost dry."

Stunned, she whispered, "How do you know that?"

"Same way I know you've got school loans to pay off, tuition due in a month and that your debit card was declined at the diner last month."

Embarrassment roared to life inside her and she felt heat crawl up her cheeks to flood her face. Bad enough that her friend Sophie knew how little money she had. Having Dave Firestone know it was almost too much to take.

The question was, *how* did he know it?

"Are you spying on me?"

He laughed. “Hardly. I had an investigator looking for Alex and, since you’re the man’s housekeeper, you got checked out, too.”

A wave of outrage crested over the embarrassment, smothering it completely. “You had no right.”

“Whether I did or not, it’s done,” he said easily, as if invading her privacy meant nothing to him. And, it probably didn’t. “The point is, you need money. I need a wife.”

“What?”

“I think you heard me.”

“You can’t be serious.” This was, hands down, the most bizarre conversation she’d ever had. A *wife?* He wanted to *pay* her to marry him?

“I don’t joke when I’m making a deal.”

He stood there, tall and gorgeous and completely at ease, as if he owned the world—and from what she knew of him, he *did* own a good chunk of it. But his attitude was so confident, so…superior. As if he knew absolutely that she would agree. Well, he had a surprise coming.

“No deal,” she said and instantly felt a sense of righteous satisfaction. Sure she was out of money and eating Top Ramen and daydreaming about hamburgers. But she wasn't so desperate that she was willing to sell herself to a man who already thought far too highly of himself. "I'm not interested in being your wife…real, temporary *or* fantasy."

"Sure you are," he said easily and gave her a half smile that tipped up one corner of his mouth and flashed a dimple at her. "You don't want to be interested but you are. Why wouldn't you be? Mia, this is a good deal for both of us."

She hated that he was right. She didn't want to be interested but she was. The whole situation was too strange. His offer was crazy. And yet… she looked around the empty living room. This place had been her first real home in too many years to count. She had cared for it and watched over it in Alex's absence. But the truth was, if he didn't come home soon, she didn't know what she would do.

The money was almost gone. Soon, she wouldn't be able to pay the monthly bills. She had no idea what she'd do then.

People in town were already speculating about

Alex's disappearance. This couldn't possibly help the situation.

"What about the local gossips?" She shook her head. "Don't you think they'll be a little suspicious of your sudden engagement plan?"

He frowned. "Hadn't considered that," he mumbled. "But it doesn't matter. In this town, the gossips love a good romantic story better than anything else. They'll glom on to our whirlwind romance and let go of suspicion."

He was probably right, she told herself. The main gossip chain in Royal was female and they were more interested in fairy-tale romantic stories than anything else. This might actually take the heat off them where Alex's disappearance was concerned.

Oh, God, she didn't know what to do.

"Think about it, Mia," he said and she could only imagine the snake in the Garden of Eden had sounded just as convincing. "This would solve both of our problems."

"I don't think so," she said, though her grumbling stomach disagreed. Still, she wasn't starving. She had a roof over her head and noodles in the pantry. And she had her pride, right?

Oh, God. Her pride was already shattered. Dave Firestone knew she was out of money. Knew how desperate she was. And he knew just what kind of temptation to use against her.

"You're considering it."

"I'm considering lots of things," she told him. "Like throwing you out, finishing my lunch and then maybe polishing the kitchen floor. Lots of options."

"So I see," he said, a slow, knowing smile curving his mouth. "Any idea which one you're going to go with?"

"I haven't decided yet," she said on a sigh.

"Let me make it easy for you, then." He moved in closer and Mia felt caught in the steady gaze of his eyes. "I'll pay you ten thousand dollars to pretend to be my fiancée until I get that deal with TexCat."

"Ten thousand—" She broke off, stunned at the offer. Just the thought of that much money made her head swim. She could pay the bills. Take care of Alex's house until he got back. She could make a payment on her tuition and finish her counseling degree.

She could buy *meat.*

"And," he said.

"There's more?"

"Yeah. Along with the ten thousand," he said, voice dropping to a low, seductive level, "I'll pay off your college loans. You could start your career out fresh. No debt."

Staggered, Mia actually swayed on her feet. That was a tremendous offer. If she didn't have to pay back school loans, she could build a life for herself much more quickly. Glaring at him, she said, "You're really evil, aren't you?"

He grinned, fast and wicked. "Just a master negotiator."

He was that, she told herself.

"Still want to polish the kitchen floor?"

She frowned at him. "Ten thousand dollars."

"That's right."

"And my loans paid off."

"You got it."

"How long would we have to pretend?"

He shrugged. "Shouldn't take more than a month."

Nodding, she tried to think clearly despite the racing, churning thoughts in her brain. "A month as your fiancée."

"Yeah."

Her eyes narrowed on him. "And what does this 'pretending' entail?"

It took a second for him to get what she meant and then he laughed shortly. "Trust me, your virtue is safe. When I want sex, I don't have to pay for it."

She could believe that. Heck, just standing next to him had her skin buzzing. He probably had women throwing themselves in his path all the time. Which made her wonder why he hadn't asked one of the no doubt *legions* of women littering his bed to be his pretend fiancée.

Maybe, she thought, none of them needed money as much as she did. Well, that was depressing.

Just to be sure of where she stood, Mia said, "Then we agree. No sex."

"Agreed."

She kept talking. "No touching of any kind. No kissing—"

"Hold on," he stopped her in midstream. "We have to convince this guy we're a real couple. So there *will* be touching. And kissing. And there will be you looking at me with adoration."

She laughed.

He frowned.

"Fine, fine," she said, waving a hand at him. "I'll be a good fiancée and the occasional touch or kiss—in public—is okay."

"Then we have a deal." He held out one hand to her and waited for her to take it. "You should come to the ranch for dinner tonight. We can work out the details there."

Nodding, Mia slid her hand into his and couldn't help feeling that just maybe she was swimming in waters *way* too deep for her.

Three

Dave pulled the collar of his dark brown leather jacket up higher on his neck and squinted as he climbed out of his 4x4. He took a deep breath, dragging the cold air into his lungs with a smile. Just being on his ranch settled him like nothing else could.

Land swept out to the horizon. He took a long look around, taking in the wooded area crowded with wild oaks. The stock watering pond shimmered a dark blue beneath the lowering sun and the grassland was dotted with Black Angus cattle. He tossed a glance at the dark, cloud-studded

Texas sky. October was rolling in cold, signaling a rough winter to come.

But he was prepared. No matter what Mother Nature threw at him, Dave was ready. He had the ranch he'd always wanted, more money than he knew what to do with and the future was looking good—except for one small fly in his proverbial ointment. But, he reminded himself, he'd found a way to take care of that, too. Who would have guessed that Mia Hughes would be the solution to his problem?

One thing he'd learned over the years, though, was that sometimes answers came when you least expected them. And he was quick enough to take advantage of opportunities when they presented themselves.

He'd worked for years to get this ranch. He'd sacrificed, wheeled and dealed and risked more than he cared to remember. But he'd finally done it. He'd reclaimed the life that should have been his from the beginning. And he'd done it in style.

Damned if he'd be defeated now.

His ranch would be a success without TexCat and he knew it. But the bottom line was they were the best, and he wanted that contract to prove his ranch was the best. It was a milestone of sorts for Dave and he wouldn't rest until he'd reached it.

Walking away from his 4x4, he tugged his hat down lower over his eyes, stuffed his hands into his jacket pockets and headed for his ranch foreman, Mike Carter. Somewhere in his late fifties, Mike was tall and lean and the best ranch manager in Texas.

"Hey, boss," he said as Dave approached. "We found those ten yearling calves we were missing huddled together in Dove canyon."

With this much open land, cattle tended to wander, following the grass. And the young ones were always straying from the safety of the herd, going where they were easy prey for wolves and coyotes. It was inevitable to lose a few head to predators every year, but Dave was glad to hear they'd recovered the stock safely this time. "Good news. You got all of 'em?"

"All but one." Mike pulled his hat off and tipped his face into the wind. "Wolves got that one. Found the signs."

Nodding, Dave frowned. The one thing he did *not* have control over was nature. If wolves wanted to pick off a calf, there wasn't much he could do about it. Losing one was hard, but they'd saved nine, so he'd have to accept that and be grateful for it.

"Fine. But I don't want to lose anymore. Let's move the herd farther from the canyons, make it harder for the young ones to wander off."

Mike grinned. "Already done. Got a couple of the boys moving cattle to the west pasture."

"Good." Dave glanced around, his gaze sweeping across his land, and he knew he'd never tire of the view. Acres of good Texas earth stretched out for miles in all directions. There were rolling hills, meadows that ran so thick with sweet grass the herd couldn't manage to eat it all. There were wooded acres of oaks, a dozen stock ponds and a couple of lakes with the best damn trout in Texas. It was everything he'd planned for, and now Dave just needed to seal the ranch's success.

"I bought some first-calf heifers this morning," Dave said, remembering the phone call he'd made before setting out to talk to Nathan and Mia.

"They'll be here by Friday and should start calving in the next couple of weeks."

"Good deal," Mike said. "We can always use new stock. But what about that new beef contract with TexCat?"

Frowning, Dave said, "I'm working on it. Should know something soon. Meanwhile, start culling the herd, separating out the stays from the gos."

"We'll do it."

When Mike went back to work, Dave told himself he should do the same. Ranch work wasn't all done outside. There were papers to go over, bills to pay, calls to make. Plus, he had a "fiancée" coming over for dinner and he'd better let his housekeeper, Delores, know.

He drove back to the main house, but rather than go inside, he walked to his favorite spot on the Royal Round Up ranch. He skirted the flagstone decking that ran the length of the sprawling ranch house, walked around the massive freeform pool and took the rough-hewn stairs to the rooftop, wraparound deck.

From that vantage point, he could see for miles.

His gaze slid across the beautifully maintained grounds, the stocked trout lake that lay just beyond the pool and then to the massive guesthouse he'd had built two years before.

The guesthouse was an exact replica of the ranch house that had been his family's until he was ten years old. Until his father had lost the ranch and then took off, leaving Dave and his mother on their own. He'd built the damn guesthouse as a trophy. A way of reclaiming the past. And as a way of giving his mom a place to call her own. A place where she could take it easy for a change. But the hardheaded woman refused to leave her small apartment in Galveston. So the completely furnished, three bedroom, three bath guesthouse stood empty.

Until Dave could change his mom's mind. Which he would manage to do eventually. Hell, he'd gotten Mia Hughes to agree to his proposition, hadn't he?

The wind pushed at him as it raced across the open prairie, carrying the scent of grass and water and *land.* His land. He felt like a damn king when he stood up here surveying the strong-hold he'd built.

He slapped both hands onto the thick, polished wood rail and leaned forward, letting his gaze move over the view. His hands tightened on the railing in front of him as he eased the jagged edges inside him by staring out at his property. Good Texas pastureland stretched to the horizon and it was all *his*. He'd come a hell of a long way in the past several years and there was more to do yet.

Landing that deal for his cattle was paramount for the rest of his plans. He wanted his ranch supplying the beef to the best restaurants and organic grocers in the state of Texas. And TexCat would help him accomplish that. Without that contract, Dave's plans would take a lot longer to come together. And if this bargain with Mia worked as he thought it would, the deal was as good as done.

Smiling to himself, he gave the railing a slap, took one last look at the vista rolling out into the distance and then took the stairs down. He'd head back to the main house and get some work done before it was time to meet with his fiancée.

Scowling, he realized it might take some time to get used to even *thinking* the word *fiancée*.

He ducked his head into the wind and muttered, "A hell of a thing to need a *wife* to make a deal."

Mia didn't know what to wear.

Was there a protocol for having dinner with a pretend fiancé who was *paying* you to pretend to love him so he could sell cattle? She laughed a little. It sounded bizarre even to her, and she was living it.

"Oh, God. I'm letting him *pay* me."

Her chin hit her chest and she took a long, deep breath to try to steady the nerves jumping in the pit of her stomach. It didn't help. Sighing, she flipped through the tops hanging in her closet and listened to the clatter of the hangers sliding on the wooden rod. She wasn't finding anything. It had been so long since she'd been on an actual *date*—she stopped short at that thought.

This wasn't a date. This was…

"I don't even know what this is," she muttered and grabbed a dark blue cable-knit sweater from the closet. Why she was worried about this was beyond her. What did it matter what she looked like? It wasn't as if she was trying to impress Dave Firestone, for heaven's sake.

"Exactly," she told herself. "This is business. Pure and simple. He didn't ask you to dinner because you swept him off his feet."

Mia laughed at the very idea. She was so not the type of woman to catch Dave's eye. No doubt he went for the shiny, polished women with nice hair, beautiful clothes and the IQ of a baked potato.

Potato.

"Oh, God, I hope he has potatoes at dinner." She sighed again. "And steak. I bet there's going to be steak. He's a rancher, right, so he's bound to like beef."

Her mouth watered and her stomach rumbled so loudly it took her mind off the nerves still bouncing around in the pit of her belly. Shaking her head, she carried the sweater out of the closet and tossed it onto the edge of her bed.

Since taking the job with Alex Santiago as his housekeeper, Mia had been living in the private suite of rooms off the kitchen of the big house.

Living room, bedroom and bath, her quarters were lavishly furnished and completely impersonal but for the few personal touches she had scattered around the place.

Mia had been travelling light most of her life, so she didn't have a lot of *things.* There were a few photographs and a ratty stuffed bear she'd had since she was a child. But mostly, there were books. Textbooks, paperback thrillers and romances, biographies and sci-fi novels. Mia loved them all and hated to get rid of a book. She'd recently treated herself to an ebook reader, but as much as she loved the convenience, she preferred the feel of a book in her hands.

"And you're stalling," she told herself as she walked to the bathroom. Staring into the mirror, she looked into her own eyes and gave herself a stern talking-to. "You're the one who agreed to this, so you're going to suck it up and do what you have to do. It's only temporary. One month and you'll have enough money to pay the regular household bills and no school loans hanging over your head. Of course, if Alex isn't found by the end of the month, then you're right back where you started. . . .” She stopped that thought as soon as it popped into her head. Alex would be found. And with the money from Dave she could pay pesky things like the water and gas and electric bills. Thank heaven Alex didn’t have a mortgage on the place because she didn’t know how she would have made the payment.

One month. She could do this. And get her life back on track.

Sounded good, she thought as she picked up the hair dryer and turned it on. She ran her fingers through her long, dark brown hair as the hot air pushed at it. Okay, she was nervous. But she could do this. How hard could it be to pretend to be crazy about Dave Firestone?

At that thought, she remembered the buzz of something…interesting she’d felt when he’d laid his hand on her arm. Thoughtful, she set the dryer down onto the pale cream granite counter and stared at her own image in the mirror. “Probably didn’t mean anything,” she assured her reflection. “I was probably just weak from hunger. Any man would have brought on the same reaction. It just happened to be Dave.”

The woman in the mirror looked like she didn't believe her and Mia couldn't blame her. It had sounded lame to her, too.

Shaking her head, she walked back to the bedroom, grabbed a pair of dark wash jeans from her dresser drawer and tugged them on over a pair of pale pink bikinis. When she had them zipped and snapped, she pulled on a white silk tank top, then covered it with the dark blue sweater. She stepped into a pair of black half boots, then walked back to the bathroom.

Her hair was still damp, so instead of the tight knot she usually wore it in, Mia quickly did up a single, thick braid that hung to the middle of her back. She didn't bother with makeup. Why pretend to be something she wasn't? There was going to be enough pretending for her over the next few weeks. Might as well hold on to *some* form of reality.

With that thought in mind, she flipped off the light and walked through her apartment. She stopped long enough to snatch up her black leather shoulder bag, then she was out the door and into her car before she could talk herself out of the craziest thing she'd ever done in her life.

An hour later, she was so grateful she hadn't changed her mind about coming.

"Steak done the way you like it?" Dave asked from across the table.

"It was perfect," Mia answered, though the truth was, she had been so hungry, if they had trotted a cow through the living room, she might have gnawed on it raw. At the moment though, she was comfortably full of steak, a luscious baked potato swimming in butter and sour cream and the best fresh green beans she'd ever eaten.

She sighed and lifted her coffee cup for a sip.

Dave was watching her, and she noted one corner of his mouth quirk.

"What's so amusing?" she asked.

"You," he admitted. "I've never seen a woman enjoy a meal so much."

She flushed a little, then shrugged. No point in pretending she hadn't been hungry. He had already checked her out, so he probably knew just how many packages of Top Ramen were left in the pantry. "Maybe you should broaden your horizons a little. Date a woman who eats more than half a leaf of lettuce."

He grinned. "Might have a point."

Her eyes met his and in the soft light of the dining room, his gray eyes looked as deep and mysterious as fog on a cold winter night. He wore a black sweater, black jeans and his familiar, scarred boots and he looked, Mia thought, dangerously good.

"I like your house," she blurted when his steady stare was beginning to make her twitch.

"Thanks," he said and glanced around the dining room. Mia did the same, taking another long look at her surroundings. Sadly, between her still unsteady nerves and the fact that she'd been so seduced by the scent of the meal, she hadn't taken the time to really get a good look at the room.

One thing Mia had noticed was that every doorway in the house was arched. There was a lot of wood and a lot of stone throughout—definitely a man's house. Even the dining room was oversized, and somehow so…male. The table could easily seat twenty. Heavy oak, the table's thick edges were covered with intricately carved vines and flowers. Each chair boasted the same carvings and the seats were upholstered in dark red leather.

A black wrought iron chandelier provided the lighting, and framed paintings of the Texas landscape dotted the walls. Her gaze slid back to meet Dave's and she felt that jump of nerves again. Well, she was going to have to get over that.

"Come on," he said, pushing up from the table and holding out one hand to her. "I'll show you around. You'll have to know the place if you're going to be my fiancée."

"Okay…" She turned her head toward the closed door leading to the kitchen.

"What is it?" he asked.

Mia looked at him. "No dessert?"

Surprised, Dave laughed and this time it was real laughter, not the sardonic smirk or the condescending chuckle Mia was more familiar with. Amazing how real emotion could completely change Dave's features from gorgeous to heart-stopping.

Oh, Mia hadn't counted on this. Okay, yes,

she'd felt that mild sizzle earlier today when Dave had touched her. But that could've been static electricity, too. In fact, she hadn't felt any interest in a man in so long, she'd begun to think she was immune.

Now was not a good time to find out she wasn't.

"Come on," Dave said again, "I'll take you on a tour, then we'll have dessert in the great room."

"All right," she said, and stood, putting her hand in his. She determinedly ignored the fresh sizzle she felt when his hand met hers. Instead, she focused on the promise of sugar in her near future.

He kept a firm grip on her hand as they walked from the dining room and Mia idly listened to the sounds of their boot heels on the tile floor. When she'd first moved in as Alex's housekeeper, she had been so impressed with the flawless beauty of his home. It was elegant and lovely in an understated way that she'd come to admire over the past couple years. But now, seeing Dave's house, she was bowled over by the sheer scope of the place.

It was lovely in a completely different way from

Alex's home. This was rustic, and as she'd already thought, completely *male* in an unapologetic, straightforward manner. The floor tiles were beige and brown with splashes of cream to lighten the feel. The walls were a mix of stone and wood and textured, cream-colored plaster. Dark beams bracketed the high ceilings and arched windows boasted leaded glass. Every door was a curved slab of heavy, dark wood that made Mia think of centuries-old English estates.

"You've seen the dining room and the great room," Dave was saying as he led her down a long hallway. "This is the main living room." He kept walking, then paused to open another door. "My office."

She caught a quick glimpse before he was moving on again and saw more dark wood, a large desk and a stone fireplace that looked as wide as her living room at home.

"This is the game room." He stopped again, swung a door open and Mia saw a huge flat-screen TV hanging on the wall, a pool table, a couple of vintage video games and a well-stocked bar.

"You've got PAC-MAN."

"Yeah." He looked at her. "I'm surprised you know the game."

"I spent a lot of time in arcades as a kid," she said and let it go at that. No reason to tell him that while her father was earning a living playing poker in bars and casinos, she was left to her own devices and had become a champion at video games.

A flicker of admiration shone in his eyes. "We'll have to have a match sometime."

They passed through the foyer and Mia glanced at the clear panes of glass arranged in a wide arch around the double front door. It was dark out, naturally, but there were solar lights lining the walkway to the circular driveway. When she'd arrived, she had noticed the number of outbuildings. There was a barn, a paddock and several smaller houses all at a distance from the main house. The Royal Round Up was a prosperous, working ranch that no doubt required dozens of employees.

The whole place was huge. Dave was even more wealthy than she had guessed him to be.

Which explained how he could offer to pay off her school loans without so much as blinking. She had no idea how to live like this. Not even how to *pretend* to live like this. Yes, she worked for Alex and he was wealthy, too, but in his house, she was the housekeeper. She wasn't expected to act as though it was her own home. To act as though living like this was second nature to her. The more she saw, the more anxious Mia became. What had she gotten herself into?

"This hall takes you back around to the kitchen," Dave said, and she glanced where he pointed. More art on the walls. More miles of gleaming tiles. She would never be able to find her way around this house. Plus, she didn't even have the kind of wardrobe the fiancée of a wealthy man would wear. She didn't fit into this world and she knew it. How could she possibly pull this off and convince anyone? Maybe, she told herself, it would be best if she just backed out of this deal right now. It wouldn't be a complete waste; she *had* gotten a terrific steak dinner out of it.

An inner voice complained that without Dave, she'd be paying back college loans for the rest of her life. But surely that was the saner approach to take. Nodding, she braced herself to tell Dave that she simply couldn't do it. She'd thank him and get out fast before she could change her mind.

Just then, he stopped in front of another door and threw it open. "This is the library."

If he continued speaking, she didn't hear him. All she could think was *books.* Acres of *books.* Floor to ceiling shelves lined with thousands of *books* ringed the cavernous room. There were couches, chairs, tables and reading lamps. There was a fireplace and giant windows overlooking the front lawn. With sunlight streaming through that glass, the room would be beautiful. The spines of the books lining the shelves must shine like rainbows, she thought, moving into the room and turning in a slow circle to take it all in.

"Finally found something to impress you, huh?"

"Hmm? What?" She glanced at him and smiled. A man who had a room like *this* couldn't possibly be a bad guy. Maybe she should rethink her earlier decision. "Oh. It's wonderful. Are you in here all the time?"

He leaned one shoulder against the doorjamb

and shrugged. "Not as much as I'd like. Usually I'm in my office or out on the property."

But he loved the room, she could tell. And this one, beautiful library was enough to convince Mia that she might be able to handle this, after all. They at least had books in common.

"Oh, if I had this room, I'd never leave it."

"Not even for dessert?" he teased.

She gave him another smile. "Okay, maybe I'd have to leave once in a while, but," she added, looking around her again at the thousands of books, "I'd always come back."

"Steak, dessert, video games and books." Dave looked at her for a long minute. "You're an interesting woman, Mia."

Weird, he probably meant, she assured herself. But that was all right. She could live with that.

She met his gaze squarely. "Well, you're a surprise, too."

"Yeah? In what way?"

"I never would have thought *you* would have a room like this."

He gave her a sardonic smile. "I should probably be insulted."

She shook her head. "Not really. I guess it's just the impression you give off."

"Which is?"

"A man who only cares about the next deal."

"That's not far wrong."

"No," she said, "I've seen this room now. So I know there's more to you than that."

He frowned a little as if he didn't enjoy her delving into his psyche, no matter how shallowly she went.

"Maybe this room is just for show," he said.

"No, again," she said and leaned out to run the tips of her fingers along the richly detailed leather spines of the closest books. "That table alongside the chair by the fire has a book on it. With a bookmark at the midpoint."

He nodded thoughtfully. "Okay, good eye."

"You can't fool me now," she told him. "Any man who can appreciate a room like this is more than he appears to be."

"Don't count on that," he said softly. Then, shaking his head, he added, "You know, I always thought you were the shy, quiet type."

"I'm surprised you thought about me at all."

"Well, then, we're both surprised tonight," he said, and stood back to allow her to pass him into the hallway. "Should be an interesting month."

"Or," she muttered as she slipped past him, her shoulder brushing across his chest, "a train wreck."

Four

"My bedroom and four guest rooms are upstairs," he said, and waited a moment before adding, "Shall we continue the tour?"

"Oh, I think I've seen enough," Mia assured him. Not only was she feeling uncomfortable about this whole thing, there was something else going on, as well. Some weird flashes of heat kept shooting through her and every time he touched her hand, she felt a buzz all the way down to her bones. No, seeing his bedroom probably wasn't a good idea.

"Your call," he said as he reached for her hand again. "But you should be familiar with the whole house. Be comfortable here. Learn your way around so you can convince anyone that you're used to being here."

"I don't know that I'm that good an actress."

Mia was really trying not to feel the heat between them, but his hand over hers was strong and warm and hard to ignore.

He was talking again, his deep voice seeming to echo off the high ceilings. "Good actress or not, you're motivated to make this happen."

"True," she said, because why deny it? They both knew the only reason she was here with him right now was because he'd made her an offer impossible to refuse. Which, really, Mia told herself, she should always keep at the front of her mind.

Anytime she was tempted to think of Dave as charming or when he seemed to really like her... she had to remember that he was simply playing a role. Getting into the whole act of pretending to be crazy about her. That, and the fact that he was clearly a master manipulator.

"So does this house come with a map?"

"You'll get used to it," he said.

"Highly doubtful," Mia countered as he led her toward the great room.

"You haven't even seen the outside yet."

"Why such a big house?" she asked. "I mean, you live here alone." She looked around. The place was gorgeous but massive. "What's the point of having so much room for one man?"

He stopped walking and studied her for a long moment. "Did you ask Alex the same question about his place?"

She laughed. "This is easily twice as big as Alex's house."

He gave her a quick grin filled with satisfaction. "It is, isn't it?"

Were men *always* competing? she wondered idly. Were they always striving to keep one pace ahead of whoever they saw as their rival?

"So there is no point to this giant house."

"It was the best," he said simply. "I always get the best."

Until now, Mia thought, wondering again why he'd chosen *her* for this subterfuge. Of course, maybe he didn't know any other really desperate women. Another wave of depression swamped her but she pushed through it to keep her mind on what was happening.

"Still think you should see my bedroom," he said.

"I don't see why."

He glanced back at her and gave her a half smile. "Because you're my loving fiancée who would be completely at ease there."

"Right." Not at ease. Not even close. Her stomach started jumping again and lower portions of her body heated to a slow boil.

In a house this size, she told herself, you could have five or six kids running around and still find acres of room to have some space to yourself. When she was a child, she would have loved a house like this. Especially that library. She would have camped out in that room and been deliriously happy.

Of course, when she was a kid, she would have been ecstatic with any house to call her own. A place where she could belong, bring friends. A room of her own to do homework in or daydream. Instead, she'd moved from hotel to motel back and forth across the country as her father followed the next poker game.

Watching Dave, she had to wonder if he was actually happy here. Or if the house was more a *trophy.* A tangible sign of success.

When they walked into the massive great room, Mia paused a moment to look around. The fire had been lit in the hearth and the snap and hiss of flames devouring wood whispered in the air. A few of the table lamps had been turned on, and pools of golden light fell across the furniture. Tan leather couches and chairs sprawled alongside light oak tables. Wide windows at the front of the house would, in daylight, afford an amazing view of the yard. Now, though, night crouched on the other side of the glass and the sea of blackness was broken only by the soft glow of the solar lights placed along the walkway.

Dave took a seat on one of the couches and reached for the white thermal coffeepot sitting on the low table in front of him.

Mia's gaze fell to the plate of brownies and cupcakes beside the coffeepot, and she walked over to take a seat within reach of the dessert tray. She picked up a napkin and a brownie and took a bite. Chocolate melted on her tongue and she closed her eyes and sighed a little in appreciation. When she opened her eyes again, Mia found Dave watching her. His gray eyes looked smokier than ever and his lips were tight. Tension radiated from him. “Is everything okay?”

Dave took a breath and blew it out again. He was suddenly rock hard and in pain. Who would have thought it? Mia Hughes wasn’t exactly the kind of woman he usually went for. There was no cleavage displayed. No short skirt to afford him a view of silky skin. No lipsticked mouth to tempt him. Not even a damn seductive smile.

And yet when she’d taken a bite of that damned brownie and made that soft groan of pleasure, his body had lit up like a lightning strike.

“Yeah,” he said shortly as he fought to get a grip. “Fine.” He poured them each a cup of coffee, then reached for a manila envelope lying on the table. Back to business, he told himself. Keep focused.

He pulled out a single sheet of paper, glanced at it then handed it to her along with a pen.

"What's this?" She took the paper but kept her gaze on his.

"Our agreement in writing. We'll both sign it so there won't be any questions later."

"A contract?"

"Easier all the way around to have everything laid out in black-and-white." Dave wasn't the kind of man to leave anything to chance. If there was one thing he'd learned over the years, it was that most people couldn't be trusted.

He took a sip of coffee and watched her as she skimmed the document.

Dave knew what it said. He would pay her ten thousand dollars up-front. All school loans to be paid off at the end of the month or the closure of his deal with TexCat, whichever came first. In return, she would feign love for him and do everything necessary to make sure this game worked.

She read it through and he saw her wince once or twice. He wondered what had brought on the reaction, then reminded himself that it didn't matter. They had a deal and he'd hold her to it.

"Questions?"

"One." She looked at him. "How do we explain to people in town that all of a sudden we're engaged? I mean, the whole point of this is to avoid gossip and scandal, right?"

He'd considered that, of course. Dave always thought through any proposition. "We'll say it's a whirlwind kind of thing. Unexpected. Passionate."

She laughed and he frowned. Not the reaction he'd expected. Outrage, maybe, or even embarrassment. But not outright laughter. "What's so funny?"

"You," she said as she shook her head and took another bite of brownie. She sighed a little and his groin tightened even more. If she had more than the one brownie, he might explode.

"No one's going to believe that," Mia told him. "I'm so not the type of woman a man like you would go nuts for."

He studied her for a long minute and had to admit that she had a point. If he'd noticed her at all over the past couple of years, it was only as Alex's housekeeper. He'd never looked beyond her quiet demeanor or the plain way she dressed and fixed her hair. His mistake, he thought now, looking into blue eyes that were the color of a Texas summer sky. He'd never noticed her full lower lip, the dimple in her right cheek or her quick wit. Mainly because he'd never bothered.

He was bothering now, though, and he sort of wished he wasn't.

"Okay, you have a point."

"Thanks very much."

He ignored the sting in her words and said, "Mainly it's the clothes. You need to go shopping."

She laughed again and that dimple winked at him. "With what? If you think I'm going to spend my ten thousand dollars on dressy clothes I won't need when the month is over, you're crazy."

"Fine." He nodded sharply. He could see her side of this. He took the paper from her, made a quick note and initialed it. "We'll make it ten thousand for you, five thousand for shopping expenses—"

"Five—"

"And your school loans. Deal?"

"Of course not! I'm not letting you buy me clothes."

"It's an act, Mia," he told her, voice firm and unyielding. "I'm paying you to play a part. I'm only giving you the props you need to make it real."

She shook her head and he sensed her pulling away. She might be sitting right beside him, but mentally she was out on the road, driving home and putting all of this behind her. So he put a stop to it.

"We agreed on this deal. This is just another facet of it. Nothing's changed but your wardrobe." He looked her over again and said, "You should go into Houston. They'll have more to offer."

"Any suggestions on what you'd like me to wear?"

He heard the sarcasm and again, he ignored it. "Tailored clothes would be best, I think. Get a couple of cocktail dresses while you're at it."

She huffed out a breath and stared at the agreement in her hand. "I don't know."

"Sign it, Mia," he said, holding out a pen. "One month and your loans are paid off and you and I go our separate ways. You know you want to, so just do it and get it over with."

She nibbled at her lower lip long enough to have Dave want to squirm just to relieve the pressure in his jeans. He'd thought the coming month would be a breeze. Now he had to wonder if maybe he wasn't signing up for a month of misery.

Although, he thought, maybe not.

Yeah, he'd told her that sex wasn't part of their deal, and it wasn't. But that didn't mean it had to stay that way. They were going to be spending a lot of time together. Giving him plenty of opportunities to seduce her and get her into his bed.

Damn, the thought of *that* had him getting even harder. Odd that Mia Hughes was hitting him so hard. Probably because she wasn't even trying. Had made a point of saying she didn't want to have sex with him.

Nothing more intriguing than a challenge.

"I really hate doing this," she muttered, then signed her name on the dotted line.

They were both committed to this path now, and there was no turning back.

* * *

Mia had no idea where to shop for the kind of clothes she needed. She'd never had enough money to worry about it before and even if she had, she didn't think she'd be comfortable paying several hundred dollars for *one dress.* Jeans, T-shirts and sweatshirts were her usual wardrobe, along with sneakers and sandals. The thought of her joining, even briefly, the kind of society that only the rich experienced would have been laughable if it wasn't so terrifying.

She was so not a part of the world Dave Firestone belonged to. How was she supposed to fool anyone into thinking any different? Not only did she not have the clothes for the part, she didn't have the attitude. She needed help and, thankfully, she knew just the place to find it.

Which was why Mia had come here, to the Royal Diner.

In June, Amanda Altman—now Battle—had come home to Royal and taken over the day-to-day running of the family diner with her sister, Pam. It hadn't been easy for the Altman sisters to get over their past and build a bridge to the future, but they'd managed it. And it hadn't taken Amanda and Nathan Battle long to rekindle their romance. Now they were married and Amanda was pregnant and driving everyone in town crazy with her decorating and shopping plans.

Mia smiled just thinking about her friend. She and Amanda had connected almost immediately when they'd met, and over the past few months they'd become friends. Since Mia didn't have many, she treasured the friends she did have.

Mia claimed one of the booths along the wide front windows that offered a view of Main Street. But instead of watching the people passing by, Mia looked around the familiar diner. It was old-fashioned, she supposed. When Amanda had come home she had upgraded a few things, though not enough to change the feel of the place.

The walls had been painted. Once a bright white, they were now a soft, cool green and dotted with framed photos of Royal through the years. The old chipped and scarred red counter was now a shining sweep of a deeper, richer red. The black-and-white-checked floors had been polished and the red vinyl booth seats had all been revamped. There were new chairs pulled up to the scattering of tables and sunshine streamed through the windows lining Main Street.

There was an old-style jukebox in the corner, though thankfully it was quiet at the moment. It was still morning, too late for breakfast and too early for the lunch crowd that would stream in by noon. At the moment, there were just a few customers, huddled over their coffees or chatting softly in small groups. The clink of silverware on plates was its own kind of music and settled the nerves that seemed to have taken up permanent residence in Mia's stomach.

This was all Dave's fault, she told herself. Waving money in front of a desperate woman was just…she frowned. Very, very smart. He'd known just how to reel her in. And now that she was in, she had to stop worrying over it. Too late to back out, Mia told herself, as she silently admitted that she probably wouldn't quit now even if she could. Just a few minutes ago, she had deposited the fifteen-thousand-dollar check from Dave that she had needed so badly. The deed was done. She could pay bills, buy groceries and find a way to hang on until Alex returned.

He *would* return, she assured herself. And now that she would be spending lots of time with Dave, maybe she would be able to discover information that would help locate Alex. Not that she believed Dave had had anything to do with Alex going missing. But he might know something and not even realize what he knew.

And… She was rationalizing her involvement in this crazy plan of his.

It was one month—and maybe not even that long, if he could land that contract for his cattle sooner. When the time was up she'd be free and clear to start her own future unencumbered by massive debt. A good thing. The heat she felt around Dave? A bad thing. That swirl of nerves erupted in the pit of her belly again and she had to fight them into submission. Not easy.

Somehow, she had to find a way to keep her hormones in check and remember that none of what would be happening between her and Dave was real.

She spotted Amanda and waved when her

friend smiled in greeting. Pam was running the cash register, and beyond the pass-through into the kitchen, Mia spotted their chef putting a plate together.

Morning in Royal, Mia thought. There was comfort here. Familiarity. Things she'd longed for most of her life, she had found here. And she would do whatever she had to to keep them. Even entering a deal with a man who was dangerously attractive.

"Brought your usual iced tea." Amanda walked up to the booth and set a glass down in front of Mia.

"Thanks." Her usual. Wasn't that a gift, Mia thought, to be so well-known in a place that she had a "usual" order.

"I'm so glad you came in this morning," Amanda said. "I've got a few pictures I want to show you."

"More baby room ideas?" Mia asked.

Amanda laughed and lovingly patted her slightly rounded belly. Mia caught the gesture and felt one sharp, swift tug of envy. Amanda had a man who loved her. While Mia, on the other hand, was going to pretend to be in love for a hefty paycheck.

"I know," Amanda said with a grimace. "I've become an HGTV zombie. I swear, Nathan's afraid to come home after work because he never knows what new project I'm going to hit him with."

"Nathan's nuts about you."

"Yeah," Amanda said with a private smile. "He really is. Which is why he didn't even flinch when I had Sam Gordon's crew break out the wall in the baby's room so they could add a connecting door to our room."

Amanda and Nathan lived on the Battlelands ranch in a house Nathan had had built a few years ago. It looked like a Victorian but it had all the modern conveniences.

"A connecting door makes perfect sense."

"It really does," Amanda agreed as she slid into the bench seat opposite Mia. "Of course, I'm also having Sam add on a balcony to our room, and Nathan was a little surprised to find gaping holes in *two* of our walls when he came home yesterday."

This is another reason why Mia had come to Amanda for help. Their lives were so different. Not only did Amanda have a home and a family to call her own, but she was a part of the very society that Mia would be pretending to belong to. The Battle family was every bit as wealthy as Dave Firestone and Amanda had found a way to not only fit in, but thrive.

Hopefully, she could help Mia do the same, however temporarily.

She took a quick drink of her tea and swallowed, pushing down the huge knot lodged in her throat. "I'd love to see the pictures of the baby's room," she said, looking up into Amanda's smiling face. "And I've got a favor to ask."

Instantly, Amanda's smile faltered and she reached out one hand across the table to lay it on Mia's arm. "A favor? Is everything okay?"

"Everything's fine, why?"

"Because you never ask for anything," Amanda pointed out. "I swear, if you were on fire, you wouldn't ask for water."

Mia blinked at the apt analogy. She hadn't realized that her friends knew her so well. But she'd learned long ago to stand on her own two feet. To not count on anyone or anything. And to never ask for help—because invariably people would see that as a sign of weakness.

Wow. Childhood issues, she told herself. Amazing how much she had held on to from when she was a girl. It was never easy to be objective about your own past and your life choices, but even Mia could see how her childhood had affected her as an adult. Heck, until the past few years, her past had kept her from even attempting to make friends. Thankfully, she'd at least been able to overcome that hurdle.

Smiling, she said, "I promise, Amanda. If I ever need water that badly, I'll *ask.*"

"Deal." Amanda waved to her sister, indicating she was taking a short break. "Okay, now, before I run to the back and get my three-ring binder with all of my decorating pictures to show you… you first. Whatever you need, I'll do it."

"Without even knowing what's going on?"

Amanda shrugged. "We're friends."

A rush of warmth spilled through Mia at those two simple words. Having a friend to count on was such a gift, she didn't think she would ever take it for granted.

"Thank you. I really appreciate it."

"I know you do, sweetie. So what's going on, Mia?"

God, she hardly knew where to begin. Cupping her hands around the tall glass in front of her, Mia started talking. She started at the beginning and told Amanda all about the reporter and Dave and the offer he'd made and why she needed to go shopping. When she finally wound down, she took a long drink of her tea and waited for Amanda to tell her she was crazy.

Instead, her friend grinned. "That is so fabulous."

"You really think so?"

"Well, come on," Amanda said, lowering her voice. "Honey, I know you hate to admit it, but you really *do* need the money."

Instantly, Mia flushed, remembering how her debit card had been refused right here at the diner just a few weeks ago. Amanda was right. She *did* need the money. And she *did* hate to admit it.

"I know things will be better when Alex comes

back…" Amanda paused and both of them were silent for a moment, thinking about their missing friend. "But for now, it's perfect. You each need something, and with this one little deal, you'll be setting up your future. How much better can it get? Plus," she added with a wide smile, *"shopping."*

Mia was still laughing when Abby Price entered the diner and walked up to the booth smiling. "What's so funny?"

"Nothing," Amanda said with a wink for Mia. "What can I do for you, Abby?"

Abigail Price was taller than Mia, with long, wavy red hair and an air of elegance about her. She also had a ready smile, a loving husband and an adorable, adopted three-year-old daughter, Julia.

"Well," Abby was saying, "you know the daycare center at the TCC is almost ready to open for business."

The day care had been at the center of a contentious battle in town for months. The Texas Cattleman's Club had been around for generations and they were pretty much stuck in the mud when it came to changes. It had only been a couple of years since they'd allowed women to become members. And now those women were spearheading the move to provide a safe, comfortable place for children to stay when their parents needed to be somewhere else.

Most people in Royal were all for it, but there were a few who were still fighting it even though it was a done deal. Before Alex disappeared, he had told Mia all about the TCC meeting in which the decision had been made to go ahead with the facility. Naturally, it had been Beau Hacket and his cronies, like the Gordon brothers, who had argued against it. Mia thought if Beau and his bunch had their way, everyone would still be driving wagons hitched up to horses. The man hated change of any kind and didn't care who knew it.

But bullies hadn't been able to stop progress, and the day-care center was nearly ready to open.

"Since everyone in town is talking about nothing else these days," Amanda said, "yeah. I know."

"Well, I was thinking," Abby said, "that we

should have a launch party, so to speak. You know, sort of an open house, to let everyone come in to see what we've done."

"That's a great idea," Mia said. "I know I'd love to see it."

"Thanks!" Abby smiled at Mia, then turned back to Amanda. "But we'll need food and that's where the diner comes in. I know you and Pam do catering and I'm thinking small sandwiches, potato salad, some vegetable platters…"

"We can do that, absolutely," Amanda told her. "Do you want to go over the menu and what you'll need now?"

"Oh, no. I've got a million things to do," Abby told her with a quick glance at her watch. "But I'd love it if we could talk it all over tomorrow sometime."

"That's perfect. Pam and I will be here all day, so come whenever it's convenient for you."

Abby bent to give Amanda a quick hug. "Thanks. Now, I've really gotta run. See you, Mia!"

And she was gone.

"Abby's pretty much a force of nature, isn't she?"

Amanda agreed. "She's always in high gear,

that's for sure. Now," she said, "let's get back to the fun stuff. *Shopping.*"

Mia laughed and took a sip of her tea. "I'm glad you think it sounds fun. I have no idea where to go or what to buy."

Amanda clapped her hands together, then scrubbed her palms. "I, on the other hand, know *just* where to go."

"Dave suggested Houston."

"Of course he did." Amanda waved that suggestion aside. "Men don't know anything. We don't have to go into the city. All we have to do is head down the street to Monica's shop."

"Monica?"

Amanda laughed a little. "Monica Burns. She's on the outskirts of town and she has this darling dress shop. Monica carries great stuff you won't find in department stores. Really different, really gorgeous."

"Why have I never heard of her before?"

Amanda cocked her head to one side. "Shop often, do you?"

Mia laughed. "Okay, no."

"Have to warn you, though," Amanda added, "she's pricey."

Pricey. Well, that's the kind of stuff she had to have and, thanks to Dave, she could afford it.

"Oh!" Amanda leaned over the table and lowered her voice. "You know what else we should do?"

"I'm almost afraid to ask. You look way too eager."

"That's because this is a brilliant idea," Amanda told her. "We should go to the day spa. Get the works."

"The spa?" Mia's voice defined the hesitation she felt over that plan. Saint Tropez was a local, upscale hair salon and day spa. Mia had never actually been inside—frankly, even if she could have afforded it, she would have been too intimidated to go in. She wasn't exactly the mani-pedi kind of girl, after all, and she hadn't gone for a haircut in years.

"You don't have to sound so horrified. I didn't suggest a trip to a torture chamber." Amanda shook her head and smiled.

"You might as well have," Mia admitted.

Her friend sat back and gave her a long look. "You said yourself you have to look the part of Dave's fiancée."

"Yes..."

"Well, sweetie," Amanda said gently, "that's going to take more than new clothes."

Mia laughed. How could she help it? "Thanks very much."

"Oh, I didn't mean it the way it sounded. I just... Okay, take your hair, for example."

She lifted one hand to the knot at the back of her neck. Her hair was neat and tidy. What else did she need, really? "What's wrong with my hair?"

"Nothing that a trim and some highlights and throwing away your rubber bands wouldn't fix."

Mia frowned thoughtfully. She kept her hair twisted and off her neck because it was easy. And, she silently admitted, because she was used to being...invisible. It was comfortable. Safe. No one noticed a woman who did everything she could to *avoid* being noticed.

But she'd been working for years to build a new life, hadn't she? Why else had she gone back to school? Worked as an intern at Royal Junior High? And if she was building a new life, did it make sense to hold on to the past? To cling to her old ways of doing things? To continue to hide when what she really wanted was to embrace the life she'd always dreamed of having?

She took a deep breath and asked, "How much do you think I should have trimmed?"

Amanda grinned. "Trust me."

Five

That afternoon at the Royal Round Up, the ranch hands were moving the herd to winter grass and Dave was happy to be on horseback joining them. Yeah, he could have stayed back at the main house and just issued orders, but running a ranch was in his blood. Nothing felt better to him than being on a horse, doing the work necessary to keep a ranch this size operating.

Every month of the year had different demands when you worked and lived off the land. In October, there was plenty to get accomplished while getting ready for winter.

Dave tugged his hat brim lower over his eyes

and guided his horse after a steer wandering off on its own. He turned the animal back toward the herd, then mentally reviewed the list of chores still to be done.

After they had the cows, bulls and steers moved to their winter field, the six-month-old calves would be separated from their mothers and weaned. Then the vet would have to come out and vaccinate them before they were turned out to the pasture along with the rest of the herd. Dave knew that a lot of the ranchers in the area turned the calves into feedlots, where they spent their days caged up in small pens with hundreds of other animals. Nothing wrong with the system, Dave supposed, but he preferred keeping his cattle free-range even if it did mean more work for the ranch hands.

His gloved hands tugged at the reins and sent his horse off to the right, where one or two of the heifers were beginning to stray. A cloud of dust hovered over the moving herd and swirled around the cowboys moving in and out of the steers with calm deliberation.

"Hey, boss."

Dave looked over as Mike Carter rode up, then drew his horse alongside. "Herd looks good."

"It does," Mike agreed, squinting into the late afternoon sunlight. "I sent a couple of the guys ahead to set up the temporary weaning pens for the calves."

"Good. If we can finish separating the calves from the cows by tomorrow, I'll have the vet come out the day after to take care of their inoculations."

"That'll work," Mike told him. "We can get the identification ear tags on them at the same time and have the work done, I figure, by the end of the week." He grinned. "Just in time for the first-calf heifers to arrive."

Dave smiled, too. "Always something, isn't it?"

"If you're lucky," Mike agreed. "By the time the doc's finished inoculating the calves, the first year heifers should be here. He can check them over at the same time. Save himself another trip to the ranch."

"Good idea," Dave said, watching as a couple of the cowboys swooped around the edge of the herd, guiding them toward the winter grasses.

There hadn't been much rain this year and the grasses were sparse. He'd already cut back on the number of head of cattle they were running, in spite of the fact the stock ponds were still full and water wasn't really an issue for the herd. The point was, the grasses had dried out and without enough rain, they wouldn't be coming back.

Ranching was always a series of strategic maneuvers. Paring down the herd, moving calves and saving breeding stock. You had to plan for weather you had no way to predict and try to outthink Mother Nature from month to month. It wasn't easy, but it was all Dave had ever wanted.

Right now, his concern was the land. Making sure it stayed healthy. Dave was thinking they needed to thin the herd again. With the first-year heifers arriving, and their calves born come spring, the ranch would be carrying more beef than the land could support if they didn't act soon. Now was the time to make that beef sale.

"We've got to get that deal with TexCat, Mike." He shook his head as the dust cloud rose even higher as if to highlight exactly what Dave had been thinking. "The grass can't support too big a herd for long."

"You heard anything from Buckley?"

"Not in a few days," Dave told him, and felt a flash of irritation. He wasn't used to not being in charge on a deal. Now he was in the position of having to wait on someone else, and Dave didn't *do* waiting. When he wanted something, he went out and got it. Hell, he thought with an inner smile, he'd gotten a fiancée when he needed one, hadn't he?

"When are you meeting him next?"

Dave frowned. "I'll set something up with him in the next week or so. Want to give him time to have our operation checked out."

"Buckley's not an easy man to deal with, but he's fair," Mike said. "He'll figure out we've got the best beef in Texas soon enough."

Dave did have the best beef around, and everyone knew it. Hell, his cowhands did everything short of singing the steers to sleep at night. The herd was free-range Black Angus. Organic, too—no antibiotics, no feedlots. He'd put his heart and soul into building this ranch, and now he had a fiancée who would convince Buckley that Dave Firestone was a settled, trustworthy man. Everything was moving as it should.

So why was he still feeling…off balance?

It was Mia.

The woman kept slipping into his thoughts. Ever since their meeting the night before, he hadn't been able to keep her completely out of his mind. And he knew why. She hadn't been what he'd expected and Dave wasn't used to being surprised. When he made a move—in business or his personal life—he went in knowing exactly what would happen. Knowing ahead of time how his adversary would react.

Mia had thrown him. Without even trying, she'd aroused him. Intrigued him. And set him up for more surprises. Which he didn't want.

"So, is your mom coming out to stay over Christmas again?"

Dave came up out of his thoughts and shot a look at his foreman. Mike's expression was hard to read, as if he were trying to be deliberately casual.

"Yeah," Dave said. "She'll be here in November, like always. Stay through the first of the year."

Mike nodded. "Sounds good."

Frowning, Dave briefly wondered why his foreman was so interested in his mother's upcoming visit. Then he shrugged it off. Bigger things to think about.

"Looks like you've got company, boss."

Mike jerked his head off to the west, and when Dave looked in that direction he saw a man on horseback headed their way. Even at a distance, Dave recognized him.

Chance McDaniel. Chance owned a thriving guest ranch and hotel on the other side of Royal. He made millions by hosting city people who wanted to pretend to be cowboys for a week at a time. Then there was the four-star hotel on the property that was a popular spot for weddings, conferences and all kinds of gatherings.

But McDaniel's Acres was a working ranch as well as a dude ranch. Chance ran some beef and horses on his land, too. The two of them often shared the work at busy times of the year, lending out cowhands and doing whatever was needed.

He was a good friend and like Dave, preferred, when possible, to be out riding a horse to doing just about anything else.

When he was close enough, Dave held up a hand in greeting. "What are you out doing?"

"Heard you were moving your beef to winter pasture," Chance said with a shrug. "Thought I'd ride over and lend a hand if you need it."

"Hell, yes, we can always use another cowboy," Dave said. "Appreciate it."

Chance grinned. "Beats being at McDaniel's Acres today. My guys are helping tourists try their hand at roping. Set up a plywood steer and they're taking turns using a lasso." Laughing, he added, "There's gonna be more than a few of them looking for aspirin tonight."

Laughing, Mike said, "It ain't easy being a cowboy." Then he nodded and moved off to join the other hands circling the slow-moving herd.

The two friends rode in silence for a few minutes until Dave finally said, "You usually enjoy watching city guys try to ride and rope. So why are you really here?"

Chance glanced at him. "Thought I'd let you

know that the state investigator's staying at my hotel."

"She is?" Dave felt like he'd just taken a hard punch to the gut. He'd heard about the FBI-trained investigator, of course. Nothing stayed secret for long in Royal, and it wasn't as if Bailey Collins was trying to keep a low profile, either.

She was working out of the Dallas office and had been looking for Alex for weeks. Dave had spoken to her once himself and he knew that she'd worked with Nathan to discover that Alex Santiago had a few secrets of his own. In fact, Santiago might not even be his real name. Questions brought more questions and there simply weren't any answers to be had. But knowing that Bailey Collins was staying at McDaniel's Acres told Dave that she wasn't going anywhere. Which meant that she wasn't finished looking into Alex's disappearance. Frowning to himself, Dave realized that though Nathan Battle might not consider him a suspect, Bailey might feel differently.

Dave looked at his friend, waiting. It didn't take long for Chance to continue.

"I'll say, the woman's gorgeous, really." He

gave a fast smile. "If you can get past what she does for a living."

"Why's she staying on?" Dave asked it, but he knew damn well why the woman was still here. A wealthy man didn't just drop off the face of the earth and not leave a ripple.

There were people asking questions. Reporters hadn't let go of the story at all. If anything, they kept digging deeper. Asking more questions, raising suspicions. Naturally, the state would want its investigator to stay put and keep gathering information.

Hell, when Alex did finally turn back up, Dave wanted to punch him dead in the face for causing all this.

"She's talking to people," Chance was saying. "She's been all over my ranch already, chatting up the cowboys, looking for any piece of information she can turn up."

"Great."

"Yeah." Chance snorted. "She questioned me once and I think she's looking for another shot at me. So far, I've managed to avoid her."

"By coming over to help your friends ride herd?"

"Doesn't hurt," he admitted.

Dave didn't blame him. He was sick and tired of talking about Alex Santiago. Hell, he and Alex hadn't exactly been friends before the man took off or whatever. Yet, ever since he'd been gone, Alex had become a huge part of Dave's life. Gossip, innuendo and scandal kept hanging over him like a black cloud threatening a storm.

And Chance had had it just as bad for a while. He'd been dating Cara Windsor until Alex had moved in on him. Then Cara and Alex had become an item and Chance was left on the sidelines. Naturally the gossips in town had run with that, painting Chance as a pissed-off lover wanting revenge. Which was laughable. Chance had liked Cara, but not enough to make Alex disappear.

"Looks to me like she plans on talking to everyone who knows Alex." He glanced at Dave. "Which would surely include *you.* I'm thinking you're going to look real interesting to her seeing as how you and Alex were rivals, so to speak."

"Great." Snatching off his hat, Dave pushed one hand through his hair, then settled the hat into place again. "Nathan just officially cleared me of suspicion and now I've got someone else coming in to set the town gossips raging again."

"Yeah, and they'll be all over it."

Disgusted and frustrated, Dave muttered, "Gonna go over real big with Thomas Buckley, too."

"That pompous old goat? He hates everything."

"Yeah, but I can't afford to have him hating me at the moment."

"The contract for your beef?"

"Exactly."

Chance nodded grimly. "Maybe this woman Bailey will be discreet."

"Won't matter," Dave said. "Once folks in town realize she's looking at me, the gossip will start up and it will reach Buckley."

"You can get Nathan to vouch for you there," Chance pointed out. "How're you going to handle the whole have-to-be-a-family-man-to-sell-to-TexCat thing though?"

"That part I've got covered," Dave said, with

just a touch of smug satisfaction in his voice. Quickly, he outlined his plan and his agreement with Mia.

Chance gave a long, low whistle. "You're clever, I give you that. But Alex's housekeeper?" He shook his head slowly. "To some—including Bailey—that might look like you're trying to buy her silence."

"What?" Dave hadn't looked at it like that at all. Now that Chance had brought it up, though, it made a horrible kind of sense.

"Hey," Chance said, "not to me! I know you didn't do anything to Alex. I'm just saying that suddenly turning up engaged to the housekeeper of a man who's disappeared might start even more tongues wagging."

He was right and Dave knew it. But the plan was set and damned if he'd back out now.

"They're gonna wag no matter what I do," Dave told him. "At least this way, they're all talking about what I *want* them to talk about. The engagement."

"It ain't easy living in a small town, is it?"

"Not by a long shot," Dave agreed. "Still, you

want to give it up and move to Houston or Dallas?"

Chance grinned. "Hell, no. Where would I ride my horse in the city? Besides, when you're *not* the center of gossip, it can be downright entertaining."

"Yeah," Dave countered, "but when the gossip's about *you,* it's a damn sight less fun."

"True."

Dave frowned. "Think I'll be spending as much time as I can out here with the cattle." He couldn't see a woman from the city hopping a horse to chase him down for an interview.

"Can't say it's a bad idea," Chance admitted. "Let's face it, Dave. You and I were the top suspects when Alex took off, and they haven't found anyone else to take our places, have they?"

"No," Dave said thoughtfully.

Nodding, Chance continued. "Y'know, when Alex *does* get back, he's got a lot to answer for."

"Damn straight, he does." Dave kneed his horse into a hard run and Chance was right behind him. A couple hours of hard work should be enough to clear their heads for a while.

* * *

Amanda didn't waste time once she'd made up her mind. Before Mia even knew what was happening, she and Amanda were at Saint Tropez being pampered.

Just walking into the day spa, you could feel tension slide from your body on a sigh. There was soft, ethereal music piped in from discreetly hidden speakers high on the pale pastel walls. There were fresh flowers scenting the air and frosty pitchers of lemon water sitting on silver trays alongside crystal goblets. The colors in the place were designed to soothe tattered nerves. Soft blue, sea-foam green and varying shades of cream covered every surface. Chairs were plush and overstuffed, lamps were dim and the aestheticians were warm and welcoming.

Since Mia had never done anything like this before, she was completely out of her element and grateful to have Amanda as her guide to the world of "girlie."

She should probably feel guilty for spending this kind of money, Mia told herself. But somehow, she just couldn't seem to drum up the guilt.

She was way too busy feeling…relaxed. For the first time in months, her mind was blissfully blank and her body was free of tension.

"You're sighing," Amanda said.

Mia did it again, then smiled. "I'm lucky I'm not just a puddle of goo on the floor. You know, I've never had a massage before and—"

"You poor, deprived girl," Amanda interrupted.

"I know, right?" Mia looked over at her friend with a smile. "It was amazing. Every muscle in my body is taking a nap."

"Oh, mine, too. Of course, since I've been pregnant, I can take a nap anywhere." She laughed a little. "Nathan swears I fell asleep standing up in the kitchen the other night."

Mia smiled to herself as Amanda continued talking about Nathan and the coming baby and their plans for the future. She was happy for her friend. Really. Amanda and Nathan had had to get past a lot of old hurts and mistrust to find their happiness now. But at least silently, Mia could admit to feeling more than a twinge of envy.

After growing up as a wanderer, she'd finally

found the place that was home. But she was still looking for the family she wanted to be a part of so badly. For the love that had eluded her all of her life.

"Mia?" Amanda's voice cut into her thoughts. "You okay?"

"What?" She jolted in her chair. "Sure. Why?"

"Because Natalie's asked you three times if you like the shade of nail polish on your fingers and toes."

"Oh!" She winced, looked at the woman sitting at her feet and said, "I'm sorry. I zoned out."

"Happens all the time here, believe me," the woman said with a knowing smile. "So, the dark rose works for you?"

Mia checked out her fingers and toes, wiggled them for effect and said, "Yes, thanks, it's great."

Another first, she thought. Mia had never treated herself to a mani-pedi before. But she wouldn't confess that to Amanda.

"Good. Now I'll get you some wine while you dry and then we'll escort you into the salon for your color and trim."

She winced at the thought of facing a haircut and highlights. A small thread of fear slid through the relaxation that held her in its grip. Before she could think about it too much, though, Natalie was back, handing Mia a glass of white wine. She'd also brought a glass of ice-cold lemon water for Amanda.

"Wine," Amanda said wistfully as she looked at her own goblet of water. "I miss wine. And caffeine."

"Yes, but when nine months are up, you'll have a baby in exchange for your sacrifice. That seems fair."

"It does," she agreed. "Though I've already told Nathan to bring a bottle of chardonnay to the hospital. I'm going to want a glass or three right after delivery."

An hour or so later, Mia was sitting in a salon chair staring into the mirror at a stranger. She smiled and the reflected woman smiled back.

Okay, there had been some nerves when Tiffany had come at Mia's head with a pair of shears. But the panic had dissolved when she'd realized that the beautiful Tiffany was only trimming and shaping Mia's long-ignored hair. But before she could admire herself, Tiffany had mixed up some color and affixed it to Mia's head with small sheets of aluminum foil.

While she sat under a hot dryer, wondering what she'd gotten herself into, Amanda had been right there, chatting and laughing with the other women in the salon. Even though Mia wasn't part of the conversation, she felt as though she were.

There was that tantalizing sense of belonging that she'd yearned for most of her life. This was her home. She had friends. She had purpose. And now...she had a fiancé. Who, she told herself as Tiffany blew her hair dry, was going to be very surprised the next time she saw him.

"You're being really quiet," Amanda said.

"Just thinking."

"About?"

"About today, mostly," Mia said with a half smile. "This was a great idea, Amanda."

"Wasn't it?" A short, delighted laugh spilled from her as she walked up behind Mia's chair and met her gaze in the mirror. "Honestly, sometimes I'm just brilliant. Of course, I'll seriously owe Pam for taking diner duty herself until our extra waitress comes in. But it was worth it."

"It was." Mia swiveled around in her chair and stood up. "I feel more relaxed than I ever have."

"Well, you look great, too." Amanda did a slow circle around Mia. "I love what she did with your hair. It's still long and it's so thick I could hate you for it..."

Mia laughed and gave her head a shake, watching in the mirror how the long, layered waves swirled out, then shifted right back into place. It was amazing. She hadn't even known her hair could *do* this.

"...and the layers. I love the highlights, too. It's still dark brown, but there's warmth mixed in there now, too."

Mia lifted one hand to slide her fingers through her hair. "It feels softer, too."

"Mia?"

A voice spoke up from the side and both women turned to look at the speaker. Piper Kindred was standing in the open doorway. "Is that you, Mia?"

"It is," she said and grinned like a fool. How fun it was to see the surprise on her friend's face and to imagine how much greater Dave's shock was going to be. "Amanda talked me into a spa day."

"And doesn't she look fabulous?" Amanda said. "Well, except for the faded jeans and the long-sleeved T-shirt. Shopping is next on our list."

Piper's curly red hair was drawn back into her usual ponytail. She wore dark blue jeans and an oversized black sweatshirt covering up a curvy figure. Her green eyes were shining and her lips were curved in a wide smile.

"Good luck with that, Mia. Amanda's always loved shopping, but I don't envy you at all."

"Exactly how I feel about it," Mia admitted.

Amanda shook her head at both of them. "And you call yourselves women. Where's your gender pride?"

"Women do more than shop," Piper pointed out with a chuckle. "Like say…work as paramedics?"

"Yes, yes," Amanda retorted with a grin. "We all know you're a paramedic and that's wonderful. But there's no reason you can't be female while you do it."

Piper winked at Mia. "I'm always female,

Amanda. I'm actually here for a haircut and a pedicure."

Amanda waved one hand in front of her face. "Hold me up, Mia. I think I might faint."

Mia laughed, delighted with the banter between the two old friends.

"Very funny," Piper drawled, then turned her gaze back to Mia. "Seriously, though, you look terrific."

"Thanks," Mia said. "The terror was well worth it, I think."

"Since she just got engaged to Dave Firestone," Amanda was saying despite Mia's look of stunned shock, "I thought it was time she knocked his socks off."

"Really?" Piper's eyes widened. "Well, congratulations. Kind of sudden, isn't it?"

"Yes," Mia said, throwing a quick frown at Amanda. "We were sort of swept off our feet."

"And now she's almost set to do even more sweeping," Amanda interrupted. "When Dave gets a look at her, it's going to blow him away."

"Hmm..." Piper glanced into the mirror at her

own reflection. "Maybe I could use a makeover myself."

"Any particular reason why?" Mia asked.

Piper shrugged and shook her head. "It's just, the work I do, the men I work with all look at me like 'one of the guys.' I think even Ryan Grant—my best friend, mind you—forgets I'm a woman most of the time."

Mia could understand that. She'd been ignored or overlooked for most of her life. At least Piper had her coworkers' respect. She wasn't invisible. But now, after experiencing the past few hours, Mia knew what the Saint Tropez salon and day spa could do for Piper.

"We could fix that," Amanda said in a tempting, singsongy voice. "Just let me know when you're ready and we'll have you buffed and polished and I would *love* to get you out of those sweatshirts you wear."

Piper laughed and stepped behind Mia as if to use her as a shield. "Down girl," she said, still laughing. "You've already got your 'project,' so stay away."

"Fine, fine," Amanda said. "But you'll be sorry.

Mia is going to be the talk of the town when I'm finished with her. You just wait and see."

"Oh, man…" Mia murmured, as nerves rose up inside her again. *The talk of the town?* She didn't know if she'd be able to handle that.

"Yep," Piper whispered. "You're toast now. Once Amanda gets going, nobody can slow her down. Good luck!"

Amanda took Mia's hand and dragged her from the room, already talking about what they would be buying at Monica's. Mia threw one last look back at Piper and was not reassured to see the other woman laughing.

Six

Mia sipped her glass of sauvignon blanc and willed the wine to soothe the nerves jittering in the pit of her stomach. Apparently, though, it was going to take a lot more than a sip or two.

She had a seat at the bar in the lounge at Claire's restaurant. The bar was as elegant as the restaurant itself. Small, round tables, candles flickering in the center of each of them. The polished mahogany bar shone under the soft glow of overhead lighting. Smooth jazz sighed from speakers tucked against the ceiling, and a long mirror backed the bar itself, reflecting the patrons seated in the room. Some, like Mia, were waiting to meet their parties and have dinner. Some were there for a quiet drink with friends.

She gave her own reflection a wry smile and still hardly recognized herself. In the deep scarlet, long-sleeved silk blouse and black slacks, she was out of her comfort zone and into foreign territory. It wasn't just the new clothes or the hair, or even the makeup she'd taken the trouble to apply, though. It was the whole situation. The subterfuge. The lies that would dominate her life for the next month.

And, she was forced to admit, if only to herself, that being around Dave constantly wasn't going to be easy, either. He was too gorgeous. Too sure of himself and far too touchable.

In just a couple of days, her life had been turned upside down. Now, instead of being curled up in her suite at Alex's house, watching TV, she was here, wearing silk, drinking wine and fighting the urge to bolt.

Being in the bar wasn't helping the situation any, either. She felt out of place, alone on her barstool. She'd never been comfortable in places like this, despite the elegance. Mia had spent too much of her childhood in the back rooms or kitchens of bars and restaurants and casinos. The clink of glasses, the murmured conversations and the smell of alcohol awakened a memory, and for just a moment or two, she was ten years old again.

The back room of the bar was small and so well lit Mia didn't need the pocket flashlight she always carried so she could read wherever she happened to be. Tonight, she sat in a corner, a glass of root beer at her side, and tried to concentrate on the magical world of Narnia.

But the poker game going on across the room from her made it really hard. Men argued and grumbled and the laughter from the women sounded sharp and brittle.

She looked around the group of men and caught her father's eye. He winked at her and Mia smiled. This was just one more poker game in a never-ending chain of them. This bar was in St. Louis, but winter was coming and her father had promised they were headed West after he got a stake from tonight's game. Vegas, he'd said. With maybe a side trip to California and Disneyland.

Mia smiled to herself and shifted her gaze back to her library book. Her father always made wonderful promises. But she had learned when she was just a little kid that she couldn't always count on them.

"How you doing, Princess?"

She looked up from her book into her father's big blue eyes. She had his eyes, he always told her. And her beautiful mother's nose and mouth. Every night before bed, her father showed her pictures of the mother she couldn't remember. The pretty woman had died when Mia was still a baby. It was sad, but she still had her daddy and that was enough.

"I'm fine, Daddy."

"Hungry?"

"Nope, I'm just reading."

"Just like your mom," he said and kissed her forehead. "Always have your pretty nose in a book." He smiled and smoothed one hand over her hair. "One of these days, sweet girl, we're gonna hit the jackpot. We'll buy us a house with a

library just like the Beast's in that cartoon movie you love. You'll have your own room you can decorate any way you want and you can go to school."

That was her favorite dream. She couldn't even imagine going to sleep and waking up in the same room every day. A house to call her own. On a nice street, maybe with trees and a swing in the backyard. And she could have a puppy, too. And the puppy would love her so much it would sleep in her bed with her. And she could go to school and have friends and every day when she came home on the bus her dog and her father would be waiting for her, so happy to be together again.

But it wasn't going to happen. Her daddy was a professional gambler and she already knew that they had to go where the games were.

So they did.

"Hey, Jack," someone called out. "You playin' or what?"

"Right there," her father answered, then leaned in and kissed the tip of Mia's nose. Whispering, he said, "Another hour or so, Princess, and we'll head back to the hotel. Tomorrow morning, we'll

get on the road early and head for Vegas. You good with that?"

"Yes, Daddy." Her father never left her alone in a motel room. Too afraid of losing her, he always said. But the truth was, Mia wouldn't have stayed even if she could have. She wanted to be where her father was. They were a team and he was all she had. They might not have a puppy or a house, but that was okay because wherever Jack Hughes was, that was home.

"That's my little good-luck charm," he said and kissed her again. "Another hour, tops."

She would have waited for him forever.

Dave grabbed the cell phone when it rang and said, "Hello?"

"Dave, did you buy me a new car?"

He smiled at the familiar voice and the note of outrage in it. "Who is this?"

"Very funny," his mother retorted. "Now explain the new Lexus that was just delivered."

"What's to explain?" he asked as he checked for traffic then loped across the street. He was headed for Claire's to meet Mia for dinner. He hadn't wanted to bother scouring the parking lot for a space, so he'd parked on the street and walked over. "You needed a new car, now you've got one."

"My old car was fine," his mother said with a sigh of exasperation.

"Key word there being *old,*" Dave told her. Then he stopped outside the restaurant, leaned against the edge of the building and let his gaze sweep the small town while his mother talked in his ear. After a long day on the ranch, he was tired and hungry and eager to get his deal with Mia started.

He'd already stopped at McKay's jewelers for a ring. Which, he knew, thanks to Erma McKay, owner and one of the top links on the Royal gossip food chain, would be all over town before he got to the restaurant. Dave smiled to himself as he remembered Erma's nose practically twitching as she'd sniffed out his story of a whirlwind romance and a surprise engagement.

He glanced up and down Main Street. It was dusk, so streetlights were blinking to life. Cars were pulled into the parking slots that lined the street in front of the shops. A kid raced down the sidewalk on his skateboard, wheels growling in his wake.

The jeweler's box in his jacket pocket felt as if it was burning through the fabric. He had never considered getting married. Or if he had, it was in a "someday maybe" sort of context. Now, even knowing the engagement was a farce and all his own idea, he felt a proverbial noose tightening around his neck. Dave hadn't exactly grown up with the best example of a working marriage, so why in hell would he be interested in tying himself down to risk the same sort of misery?

"David, this has to stop. You can't keep buying me things," his mother said flatly, and that caught his attention.

"Why not?"

"Oh, for heaven's sake, enjoy your money. Go buy something fun for yourself."

He had, he thought. He'd bought himself a fiancée, but not being an idiot, he didn't say that out loud. "Mom..."

"I'm serious, David. If you want to give me something, make it grandchildren."

Dave shook his head as a woman with two kids, one of them howling as if he was being tortured, went past. Kids? No, thank you. "Cars are easier. Just enjoy the Lexus, Mom."

"How can I when I know you're spending your money on *me?*"

"I'm doing it for myself," he said, knowing just how to get gifts past his too-proud-for-her-own-good mom. "I worry about you and if you're in a safe, new car, that's at least one thing I don't have to worry about."

She sighed on the other end of the phone and Dave knew he'd won this round. His mother had worked her ass off taking care of him and seeing that he got all of the opportunities she could manage. And if he had his way, she'd be treated like a damn queen now. Even if he had to fight her to make it happen.

"I don't know where you got that hard head of yours," she said in a huff. "But I'm out of time to argue with you. I'm meeting Cora for dinner, so I've got to run."

"Me, too. I've got a dinner date."

"Ooh." His mother's radar instantly went on alert. "Who is she?"

Dave grinned. "Have a good time, Mom."

"Fine, fine." Exasperation coloring her voice, she said, "You're an evil son to not tell me about this woman, but you have fun, too."

Still smiling, he hung up, stepped into Claire's and headed directly to the bar, knowing that Mia would be there waiting for him, since he was late. That thought wiped the smile from his face. Dave didn't do late. He was always on time, always in control, and the fact that that control had started slipping the minute he got involved with Mia hadn't escaped him.

He scanned the bar quickly, thoroughly, and didn't see her. Had she stood him up? Changed her mind about the whole thing? Well, damned if he'd let her back out now, he told himself. They had a plan and they were going to stick to it, even if she…

He caught a woman's gaze in the wide bar mirror and his breath left him in a rush. It was her. Mia. And she looked…amazing.

Mia was, quite unexpectedly, Dave told himself, the most beautiful woman he'd ever seen. How could this stylish, sophisticated brunette sitting alone at the bar possibly be Mia? Where was the tidy bun at the back of her neck? The unadorned eyes and the naked lips? Admiration mingled with desire inside him and frothed into a dangerous mix. He took a moment to catch his breath, and to enjoy the view. Her legs looked impossibly long in her sleek black slacks and he found himself wishing she'd worn a damn dress so he could get a good look at those legs.

He had to wonder if that glance they'd shared in the mirror had displayed the hunger in his eyes. Damn, he hadn't had a rush of pure, unadulterated lust like this in— Hell, he couldn't even remember the last time he'd *wanted* anyone this badly.

If he hadn't already decided to seduce her into his bed, seeing her tonight would have made the decision for him. He was hard and eager and ready to say screw dinner and just whisk her back to the ranch. Unfortunately, he thought, she was going to take some convincing. Still, there was nothing he liked better than a challenge.

"Mia?"

She blinked, and her eyes lost that faraway look and focused on him in the mirror. Her lips curved and his groin tightened.

Damn, it felt like a fist to his chest. Amazing what a woman could do to a man with a single look and a knowing smile. Were her eyes always that big? he wondered. Were they really so deep it seemed he could dive into their depths and drown?

"Dave?" Her voice shook him. It was deep, filled with concern. "Are you okay?"

Get a grip. "Yeah. Fine. Just…" His gaze swept her up and down. "Stunned. You look beautiful, Mia."

She actually flushed, and until that moment, Dave would have bet cold hard cash there wasn't a woman alive who could still do that.

Something fisted in his chest and breath was hard to find. He had to regain the upper hand here. Fast.

"Hope you didn't wait long." Not an apology, he assured himself. Just a statement.

"No." She gave him a curious look, as if she

was wondering why his voice had suddenly shifted to cool and businesslike.

Well, hell, if she knew how he'd had to fight for that dispassionate tone, she'd have all the power here, wouldn't she?

"Are you ready for dinner?"

"Yes, but they haven't called our table yet and—"

"My table's ready when I am," he told her.

Both of her perfectly arched eyebrows lifted on her forehead. "Well, I hope you use your power for good instead of evil."

He laughed shortly. He hadn't expected to actually *enjoy* Mia's company. She was just full of surprises. So, to continue her comic book theme, he said, "With great power comes great responsibility."

She gave him a wide smile as a reward and lust roared up inside him, hotter than before. Shaking his head, he told her, "Leave your drink. We'll have champagne at the table."

"Champagne?" she asked as she took his hand and slid off the bar stool. "Are we celebrating?"

"Shouldn't we be?" he asked, catching her soft,

floral scent as she moved closer. "We're engaged, right?"

"Yes," she said after a moment or two, "I guess we are."

Her fingers curled around his and Dave felt heat slide through him so fast it was like a sudden fever.

But fevers burned themselves out fast; he'd do well to remember that.

He led her through the bar to the restaurant, where the hostess recognized him instantly and picked up two menus. "Welcome back, Mr. Firestone. If you and your guest will follow me..."

The young woman headed into the interior of Claire's, where the lights were dim and the pristine, white linen tablecloths shone like snow in the darkness. Candles flickered madly, sending shadows dancing across the walls. Couples and larger groups sat at the tables and booths, their low-pitched voices no more than white noise. The same smooth jazz from the bar sighed into this room as well and gave the whole place a sense of intimacy.

Dave had brought a few dates here before, but

mainly he used Claire's as a place to talk business. The waitstaff was attentive but not cloying, so you had plenty of time to talk without being interrupted constantly.

Tonight, though, was a different kind of business.

And damn if he'd risk his future because his rock-hard body was screaming at him.

With his hand at Mia's back, he steered her through the maze of tables and chairs. The cool silk of her shirt and the heat of her body mingled together to twist his guts into a knot that tightened with every breath.

The hostess showed them to Dave's usual table, a secluded booth at the back of the restaurant, and once they were seated she moved off, leaving them alone. Mia picked up her menu immediately and Dave smiled. It was actually nice to be out with a woman who liked to eat. Most of the women he spent time with never ate more than a salad and, even with the dressing on the side, they seldom finished their meal. A little irritating to pay for food that ended up being tossed.

She looked at him over the top edge of her menu. "I've never been here before. It's lovely."

"Yeah," he said, glancing around. "I suppose it is."

He'd become so accustomed to Claire's that he hadn't bothered to even notice his surroundings in longer than he could remember. Now, seeing it through Mia's eyes, he saw that it was more than a handy meeting spot. It was refined, yet casual enough to be comfortable.

In the candlelight, Mia's skin looked like fine porcelain, her eyes reflected the dancing flame in the center of the table and her hair fell in long, soft waves over her shoulders. The top two buttons on her silk blouse were undone, giving him a peek at smooth skin that only made him want to see more.

Sure, he'd been attracted before, but this Mia was at a whole new level. She'd surprised him, and that wasn't easy to do. He wondered what she was thinking as she stared back at him and realized that it was the first time he'd even cared what a woman was thinking. She was hitting him on so many different levels, it was almost impossible to keep up.

To get his mind off what his body was clamoring for, he said, “When I walked in tonight, you looked a million miles away.”

“What?” she frowned. “Oh.” Shrugging a bit, she said, “I was just remembering.”

Curiosity pinged inside him. “Remembering what?”

“My father,” she said simply.

He hadn’t expected that, either. Her voice was soft, filled with fond affection that he couldn’t identify with. He laid the menu down since he didn’t need to read it anyway. Dave knew what he was going to order. Same thing he always got. Steak. Potatoes.

Instead, he focused on Mia. Her eyes drew him in and he tried to figure out what exactly she’d done differently. Makeup, sure. Eyeliner and a soft brown shadow on her lids. But it was the emotion in her eyes that grabbed at him. “Where is he now?”

“He died about ten years ago.”

"Sorry," he said and meant it because he could see what the man's loss meant to her.

"What about you? Is your father still alive?"

He stiffened. See? He told himself. This was why he rarely took notice of someone else's life. It inevitably turned around on him. "No idea."

"What do you mean?"

"He walked out on my mom and me when I was ten. Never saw him again."

Her eyes instantly went soft. "Oh, Dave, I'm sorry."

He didn't want sympathy. Didn't need it. He'd long ago left behind the boy who'd missed his father. Dave had done just fine without the man who'd walked out on his responsibility. His *family.*

"I don't know what to say," Mia murmured.

"Nothing to say," Dave assured her, and wished the waiter would bring the champagne he'd ordered ahead of time. "Long time ago. He left. We lost our ranch and my mother became a cook for the family who bought the place."

His voice was clipped, cool, giving away nothing of the still-hot bubble of rage that these memories brought to him. Even after all these years, Dave could feel the helplessness that had gripped him as a boy.

Watching his mother work herself to the bone as an employee in what used to be her home. Hearing her cry at night and knowing there was nothing he could do. Hating his father for walking away, and yet at the same time, praying every night that he would come back.

But he didn't. And Dave had grown up quickly. He'd made a vow to become so rich no one would ever be able to take away what was his again. He would take care of his mom and make sure she never had to work for someone else.

And he'd done it.

Made good on his promise to himself. Made himself into a man others envied. And he wouldn't stop now.

Mia was still staring at him, and he could see hesitation in her eyes. As if she was arguing with herself internally about whether to offer sympathy or congratulations on what he'd become. He'd save her the question.

"The past doesn't matter."

"You really believe that?" she asked.

"I do. All that counts is now and the future you build."

"But it's the past that made us who we are."

"You're right. But you can't change the past, so why think about it?" he asked.

"To learn from it? To remember the good things?"

Their waiter showed up at their table, ending their conversation as he carried a silver ice bucket with a chilled bottle of champagne inside. They were silent as the waiter popped the cork and poured a small amount into a wineglass for Dave to try. When he approved it, both glasses were filled and the waiter took their orders.

Dave smiled to himself as Mia ordered the same thing he had. Steak and a baked potato.

"Still hungry?" he asked, before she could return to the conversation about the past. He was done looking backward.

She shrugged. "No point in pretending not to have an appetite. This isn't exactly a date, is it?"

He laughed a little. "So women only pretend to not be hungry when they go out?"

"Sure," she said. "I bet every skinny woman in the world goes home after a date and dives into her fridge when no one's looking."

"Speaking from experience?"

"Not really," she admitted with a shrug. "It's been a *long* time since I was on a date."

"I don't get that." She was gorgeous, funny and smart enough to know a good deal when it was presented to her. Why wouldn't men be interested?

She picked up her champagne and sipped at it. A slow smile curved her mouth when she swallowed and a twist of need tightened Dave's guts. Damn, she was a dangerous female.

"I haven't had time for dating, really," she was saying. "Getting my degree has taken up all my time, and then there's taking care of Alex's house to be able to pay for school. Not to mention the interning at Royal Junior High. So, dating? Not really a priority."

"I can understand that," he said, impressed with her work ethic and determination to carve out her life on her terms. "You have a goal, you do what you need to do to make it happen. I did the same thing."

"How do you mean?"

The restaurant was quiet, just the hum of low-pitched conversations and the background music that drifted in and out of notice. The candlelight created an air of intimacy, so Dave could have believed that he and Mia were the only two people in the room. Maybe that was why he'd told her what he'd never discussed with anyone else before.

He took a sip of champagne and thought how different his life was now than it had been just ten years before. Back then, it was cheap beer and big plans. He started talking, his voice hardly more than a hush.

"I worked my way through college, like you." His fingers, curled around the stem of the wineglass, tightened slightly as memories rushed through his mind. He never looked back, so when he did, it jolted him. "Took whatever job I could. Paid for school, and saved whatever else I could. In my geology class, I met a guy, Tobin Myer."

"Interesting name," Mia said.

"Interesting guy," Dave countered. "He didn't have many friends. Spent most of his free time exploring, doing tests on vacant land."

"What kind of tests?"

He chuckled and relaxed into the telling. He wasn't sure why talking to Mia was so damn easy and didn't think he should delve too deeply into that. "Y'know, even now, I couldn't tell you. Tobin could, of course. He could talk for hours about mineral deposits, shale, oil traces…the man was born with dirt in his blood, I swear."

"You liked him."

Dave glanced at her. "Yeah. I did. We were both loners. I didn't have time for friends and parties. Tobin was too far out there for anyone else to give a damn about him so… Different reasons, but we were both still alone. Maybe that's why we connected. Anyway…" Enough of the psychological B.S. "Tobin found a piece of land that had him excited. Said the signs of mineral deposits were through the roof. But he needed a backer. Someone with enough money to buy the land and be his partner in developing it."

"You."

He nodded. "Me." Hell, even he found it hard to believe that he'd taken the risk, spent the money it had taken so long to put together. "I took my savings and invested it in Tobin and that parcel of land."

"I'm guessing," she said, lifting her wineglass, "that since we're sitting here drinking this lovely champagne and you're paying me an extraordinary amount of money for a few weeks' time, Tobin was right."

"Oh, he was better than right," Dave told her. "That piece of land was worth a fortune."

"So you sold it?"

"No, we leased it to a huge oil and gas company outside of Dallas," he said. "They wanted to buy, of course, but instead we kept the title, and in exchange they paid us a boatload upfront and a hefty royalty every quarter."

"Your idea?"

"Absolutely." He grinned, remembering his first big deal. He'd stood his ground with the big company, kept Tobin from having a stroke due to anxiety and he'd pulled it off. "Tobin would have taken their first offer, he was so excited to be right about the land."

Dave could still feel the rush of satisfaction that had filled him when he and Tobin had made the deal. They'd each received a small fortune on signing and the royalty checks over the years had only gotten bigger. That was what had given him the means to buy his ranch and build his house, and was the seed money for everything that had come to him since.

"Do you still see Tobin?"

He looked at her. "Yeah, I do. He's based out of Dallas now, but spends most of his time in his jet, checking out land all over the country. Still following that love of dirt."

"And you're still partners."

"Ever hear of MyerStone Development?"

"Actually, yes. They're in the business section of the paper a lot and—" She stopped and smiled. "You and Tobin."

"Me and Tobin," he said, and lifted his glass in a salute to his partner.

"So the past can be nice to look back on."

He caught her eye and nodded. "Touché."

They ordered their meal, and throughout dinner, they talked of everyday things. What was new in Royal. The fact that there was no news about Alex, and then, finally, just how they would convince Thomas Buckley that they were a couple.

The longer he was with her, the more Dave figured he had the answer to a lot of problems. Over cake and coffee, he made his move.

"I think you should move into the ranch with me."

Seven

Mia froze with the last forkful of cake halfway to her lips. "What?"

She looked like a deer caught in headlights. Good. He preferred her off balance. This would all work much better if he could keep Mia dancing in place just to keep up with him.

"Finish your cake," he urged. "You know you want to."

She popped the piece of double-chocolate lava cake into her mouth and chewed frantically. While she was quiet, Dave went on.

"Think about it for a minute. We're engaged. We'll be meeting with Buckley out at the ranch anyway. It'll be handier with you there."

She swallowed, waved her fork at him and argued, "But you told me that Buckley is really conservative. He probably wouldn't approve of us, well, living together."

"We're engaged."

She took a breath, blew it out and reluctantly set her fork down.

"Which reminds me," Dave said, reaching into his pocket for the jeweler's box.

When she saw the dark red velvet, her eyes went wide and she dropped both hands into her lap. "What did you do?"

"Mia, no one's going to believe that a man like me proposed without a ring."

Her eyes met his and he could see nerves shining back at him. Again, good. If her mind was whirring in high gear, she wouldn't be thinking clearly about much of anything.

"I don't know…"

"We're already in this. The ring is just a symbol of our bargain."

"A symbol." She took another long, deep breath, then grabbed her fork again and scraped it across the dessert plate, catching every last drop of the chocolate sauce. She licked the fork clean and had zero idea what watching her tongue move across the tines was doing to Dave.

"It's just a piece of jewelry," he said and flipped the box lid open.

She gasped and he smiled. Eyes wide, she stared at the ring and slapped one hand to her chest as if to hold her heart in place. "You can't be serious."

Pleasure filled him. Her expressions were so easy to read that he could see that she both wanted the ring and wanted to run. When she reached out a hesitant finger to touch the five-carat diamond, he knew he had her.

Her fingertip slid across the wide surface of the diamond, then dropped to follow the smaller, channel-set diamonds that surrounded it. After a long minute or two, she lifted her gaze to his.

"It's gigantic."

"It sends a message."

"Yeah. 'Here I am, robber! Take me!'"

"In Royal?" He laughed, shook his head and plucked the ring from the box. Sliding it onto her ring finger before she could pull her hand back, he said, "What it will say to everyone here is, Mia belongs to Dave."

"Belongs."

She whispered the word, but he heard it. And just for a second, that imaginary noose tightened. He ignored the feeling and focused on the plan.

Her gaze fixed on the ring for a long moment before meeting his eyes again. "I'll wear the ring—"

"Good."

"But as for moving in with you—"

"It makes the most sense."

"But I have to take care of Alex's house."

"Alex isn't there," he reminded her quietly.

"I know but—"

"And the longer he's gone, the more intrusive the reporters are going to get," he went on. "Right now, most of them are being stopped at the gate. But a few have gotten through to harass you."

"True."

"More will come. Especially once word about us gets out. They'll start speculating about us getting together. Why not be at my place? No reporter will be able to reach you there, and you can check on Alex's house whenever you want."

"I don't like leaving Alex's house," she admitted. "What if he calls? What if he needs help?'

Frowning, Dave paused and thought about it before saying, "We'll have the phone company forward calls to my place. Good enough?"

She was thinking about it. He could see her working through internal arguments, trying to decide what she should do. But he'd have his way in this.

Having her at the ranch would cement their "engagement" for everyone in town and Thomas Buckley. More than that, having her in his house would speed up the seduction—which he was really interested in. Just sitting across the table from her was making him crazy.

Every time she chewed at her lip or took a deep breath, Dave felt a slam to his center. Mia Hughes was going to be his. On his terms. Soon.

"Mia, you're living alone in that big empty house, and there's no reason for it," he reminded her. "For the next few weeks, move in with me. Take a break."

She laughed. "A break?"

"Yeah. No house to clean, no worries."

"*You'll* worry me," she admitted.

"Me? I'm harmless."

She laughed again, and he liked the sound of it. "You are many things," she said, "but harmless isn't one of them."

"Not afraid of me, are you?"

"Said the big bad wolf," she murmured, then shook her head. "No. I'm not afraid of you, Dave. I'm just..."

"...going to agree."

"Do you always get your way?"

"Always," he said.

She looked at the ring, then him and finally said, "Then I guess you win again. Okay. I'll move in."

"That wasn't so hard, was it?"

"You have no idea."

"Here," Dave said, sliding his untouched chocolate cake across the table toward her. "You look like you could use this."

She picked up her fork and dug in. "Thanks."

After a week at the Royal Round Up Ranch, Mia was no more at ease than she had been the day she'd arrived. If anything, her nerves were stretched a little tighter. Royal had been buzzing about their engagement for days. Whenever she went into town, she was stopped a half dozen times on Main Street with people wanting to talk about her "romantic, whirlwind engagement." Which only made her feel like a cheat. And if there's one thing her father had taught her, it was that "cheating is the coward's way."

She hated lying. Hated playing a part. And really hated thinking about what everyone in town would be saying when her engagement ended.

But that was a worry for further down the road. Right now, even though it wasn't easy, she was grateful to be at the ranch because Dave had been right. The reporters were even more intrusive than before, though none of them could get to her here at the Royal Round Up.

She steered her old Volkswagen Bug through the gates of the ranch and waved at the guard Dave had posted there. No reporter could get past that guard, and if anyone tried to just hop a fence and cross the ranch, they'd get lost long before they made it to the main house.

Smiling to herself, Mia drove down the winding road toward the ranch house, her mind wandering as she traveled the now-familiar route.

It had been a weird week. Oh, she was used to his house now, had even learned her way around. And in spite of its size and innate elegance, it was a homey place. Warm and welcoming. Her bedroom, directly across from Dave's, was bigger than her entire suite of rooms at Alex's house. And she was getting very used to waking up to a spectacular view of Dave's ranch. The land stretched out forever, marked by stands of wild oaks and stock ponds. It was quiet, as it could only be in the country, and at night, the sky was velvet, covered by a blanket of stars so thick it took her breath away.

It wasn't her surroundings making her nervous.

It was Dave.

And it wasn't as if he'd gone out of his way to make her jumpy. On the contrary, he'd done nothing but be very nice. Thoughtful, even. They had dinner together every night and spent hours in the library she had loved from the moment she first saw it. He took her on rides around the ranch and introduced her to his mare, due to deliver her foal any day.

Every time she turned around, there he was. Gorgeous. Warm. Sexy. He was turning her inside out and she had the distinct feeling he was doing it on purpose. That he knew by his constant attention he was wearing down her resistance. Seducing her.

And damn if she wasn't enjoying it.

It was a bad idea, though. Mia knew that. This wasn't going to be her home. He wasn't going to be hers for any longer than it took to make the deal he wanted so badly. Nothing about their relationship was real. Except the wanting. And the desire that thrummed inside her all the time was as insistent as a heartbeat.

But if this was seduction, it was the long way around. He hadn't even tried to kiss her.

"Why not?" she muttered, then glared at herself in the rearview mirror.

When this whole deal had begun, she'd made a point of saying that sex wouldn't be a part of it, so why was she…disappointed that he was keeping to their bargain?

"Because you can't stop thinking about him, that's why," she told herself and gritted her teeth as her car hit a bump on the gravel road.

That was the simple truth. She thought about him all the time. And the fact that he was so determined to keep his distance was driving her a little crazy.

"Which is just wrong and I know it," she said aloud. It wasn't as if she was a highly sexual woman, after all. She'd been with exactly two men in her life, and neither one of those occasions had been worthy of mention. There hadn't been fireworks. The angels hadn't sung.

So why was she so hot and bothered by the thought of Dave?

"Oh, for heaven's sake." The spectacular house rose up in front of her and she drove on, past the circular driveway that curved around the house. Instead, she parked her car closer to the barn. Mia just couldn't bring herself to park her beater car in front of that gorgeous house. It would be like seeing a pimple on the face of the Mona Lisa.

She looked through the windshield and saw a couple of the ranch hands at the paddock, where

Mike Carter was putting a young horse through its paces. Dave was there, too, arms hooked over the top rail of the fence and one booted foot propped on the lower rail. Over the past week or so, she'd discovered that the Dave who lived and worked at the ranch was a wildly different man than the cool, focused businessman she'd first known. It was as if he kept his soul here at the ranch and without it, he was a different man.

Unfortunately for her, she'd been attracted to the hard, distant businessman…but the rancher was unbelievably hard to resist.

Mia sighed, stepped out of the car then reached back in for her bags and the small blue glass vase that held three daisies and a red carnation. She looked at the bedraggled flowers and smiled. A grocery store special, they couldn't have cost more than five dollars and they meant more to her than two dozen roses would have.

"Mia!"

She turned at the sound of her name and saw Dave striding toward her. Late afternoon sun was behind him, and her breath caught in her chest as she watched him approach. His hat was pulled low on his forehead. He wore a blue work shirt, the sleeves pushed up to his elbows, and faded jeans that clung to his long legs and stacked on the tops of his scarred brown boots.

Dave Firestone was the kind of cowboy that would make any woman's heart beat just a little faster than normal. So she really couldn't be blamed for enjoying the view, right?

When he was close enough to reach out and touch her, he stopped, glanced at the flowers she held and smiled. "You want to tell me who's giving my girl flowers?"

His girl. Something warm curled in the pit of her stomach and she was forced to remind herself that he didn't mean it. Just part of the game they were playing. The ranch hands were close by and no doubt watching them, so he was playing to his audience.

"I told you today was the last day of my internship at Royal Junior High..."

"Not even the end of the semester, was it?"

"No. The school board makes fall internships short and then does follow-ups come spring. Gives us more time to devote to schoolwork."

"Okay..."

"Well, two of my kids bought me these," she said, glancing down at the flowers that meant so much to her.

"Nice kids," he said.

She looked up at him. "They really are. I'm going to miss them."

He moved in closer. Close enough that she caught the scent of his aftershave still clinging to his skin. Her heartbeat sped up in response.

"You'll see them all again in the spring. And then again after you get your degree and start working there full time."

Since she still had a few months of school left and there was no guarantee of a job when she was finished, Mia could only hope he was right.

"You were late getting home," he said. "I was worried. Thought maybe this...*car* of yours finally gave up the ghost."

She frowned at him. Okay, her old VW wasn't exactly a luxury ride, but it was loyal, she knew all of its quirks and as long as she added a quart of oil a week, it kept running. It fired right up every morning, and it got her where she needed to go and that was enough for her. Mia didn't have enough money to think about making a new-car payment every month. "Don't make fun of my baby."

He shook his head. "Nothing funny about this car. It should have been junked years ago."

As if he could hear her thoughts, he changed the subject. "Leave your bags here," he said and scooped everything but the flowers from her arms, then stacked them on the hood of the car. "There's something I want to show you."

Excitement shone in his eyes and that half smile of his that she loved so much was tipping up one corner of his mouth. He was irresistible. She set the vase of flowers down on the hood. "What is it?"

"You'll see." He caught her hand in his and headed for the barn.

Mia had to hurry her steps to keep up with his long-legged stride. The warmth of his hand against hers simmered in a slow heat that slid through her system to settle around her heart.

The men gathered at the paddock called hello to her as they passed and she smiled, enjoying the sensation of being part of ranch life—even if it only was temporary. With that sobering thought in mind, she followed Dave into the shadow-filled barn.

It smelled like hay and horses and she heard a shuffling sound from animals shifting position in their stalls. Dave led her to the far stall, then pulled her close to look over the edge of the door.

"Oh, my..." Mia's heart twisted in her chest. Dave's mare, Dancer, was nuzzling a brand-new foal, still shaky on its impossibly long, thin legs.

"Happened just a couple hours ago," Dave whispered, his breath warm against her ear. "Dancer came through like she'd done this a hundred times before."

"I'm so glad," Mia said, wrapping her arms around him for an instinctive hug. She knew how much the horse meant to him. He'd even been planning to have a vet attend the birth because he didn't want to take chances with the mare's life.

And that endeared him to her. He might pretend to be cold and shut off, but the truth was, he had a big heart. He was just careful whom he showed it to.

"Yeah," he answered, looking down into her eyes as his arms closed around her, drawing her even closer. "Me, too. I raised Dancer, so she means a lot to me."

"I know." She couldn't look away from his fog-gray eyes. She held her breath, afraid to speak, afraid to shatter this sudden shift into intimacy.

His gaze moved over her face like a caress. "It's weird, but I was anxious for you to get home, so I could share this with you."

"Really?"

"Yeah." He lifted one hand to cup her cheek. "Wonder what that's about?"

"I don't know," she said, "but I'm glad."

"Me, too," he said, and bent his head to hers.

She was dazzled with the first brush of his lips against hers. Sighing, she leaned into him and he held her tighter, pressing her body along the length of his.

Mia was lost, spiraling away into the heat and desire burning inside her. She forgot all about where they were. The barn and the horses faded away. The voices from the cowboys outside silenced and it was just her and Dave, locked in a moment that filled her with pleasure despite a tiny, tiny touch of worry.

When he parted her lips with his tongue and the kiss deepened into something amazing, the worry dissolved under an onslaught of emotion so thick and rich that Mia's mind shut down completely. She leaned into him, her arms tightening around him, her tongue tangling with his in a wild dance of a passion she'd never felt before.

Their breath mingled, their bodies pressed together and Mia heard Dave groan as he claimed her again and again. His hands swept down to the hem of her shirt and slid underneath it. The touch of his hands against her bare back was magic and she suddenly wanted more. Needed more.

But he tore his mouth from hers and left her struggling to catch her breath, fighting to find her balance. She leaned her forehead against his chest and shivered. "Why did you stop?"

He chuckled and his voice sounded raw and strained when he answered, "Because we're in a damn barn, Mia. With my ranch hands right outside that door. If we're gonna do this, then we're gonna do it right."

He paused, lifted her chin until he could look into her eyes and asked, "We *are* gonna do this, right?"

There was her out. Time to snap out of this sexual haze and remember what she was doing here. Who she was with. And why. He'd just handed her the chance she needed to reach for calm, cool logic and call off whatever it was that was happening between them. She should be grateful. Should be smart. Should tell him, "No, we're not."

"Absolutely," she said. "When?"

"I'm thinking *now*."

"Oh, good idea." Mia was still trembling. Still shaking from needs awakened and screaming inside her. "Where?"

"Your room. Fifteen minutes."

"Right. Fifteen minutes." She took a breath and blew it out. "Why so long?"

He laughed and she did, too. This was ridiculous. She was acting crazy. She'd never done anything like this before. It was so out of character for her. And she liked it a lot.

"Because," he said, letting her go long enough

to adjust his jeans, "I'm not going to be able to walk across that yard for at least ten minutes."

She flushed, then grinned. Wow. She'd never done that to a man before. Had him so hard he wasn't able to walk. It felt...great.

"Okay, then," she said, taking another breath, which only succeeded in fanning the flames licking at her insides. "I'll be waiting."

His gray eyes burned with an intensity that was new to her as he promised, "I'll get there as fast as I can."

Nodding, Mia scuttled out of the barn, waved to the guys in the paddock and hurried toward the house. She stopped at her car long enough to pick up her things, then she practically ran to the ranch house and the staircase that led to her bedroom.

Mia didn't have much time. She raced up the stairs, praying she wouldn't run into Dave's housekeeper as she went. She hit her bedroom at a dead run and pulled her clothes off as she hurried across the room to the attached bath. She hopped into the shower and thanked heaven she'd shaved her legs the day before. When she was finished, she dried off and slipped into the heavy, white robe hanging on the back of her door, tying the belt with shaking hands.

She was taking a step here. A big one. She hadn't meant for her relationship with Dave to go this far, but now that it had she wouldn't regret it. Instead, she was going to grab at the chance fate had handed her. For years, she'd been locked away in schools, libraries, tucked up in her suite of rooms at Alex's house. *Life* had been passing her by and she'd hardly noticed.

Mia took a deep breath and slapped one hand to her belly in a futile attempt to quell the butterflies swarming inside. She hadn't once, in the past few years, had so much as a date. She'd been too focused on her future to enjoy her present.

Well, today that stopped. Today, Mia Hughes was going to take the time to live a little. To be with a man who *wanted* her. Whatever happened tomorrow, she'd simply have to deal with it, because she wasn't going to back away.

Mia sat down on the edge of her four-poster bed and, to distract herself from the nerves of waiting, glanced around the room that had become so familiar over the past week. The whole house was golden oak and rough-hewn stone, and her room was no different. There was a deeply cushioned window seat below the arched bay windows that overlooked the backyard. The view was of rolling green grass, stands of live oaks and ponds for the Black Angus cattle that wandered the fields. A stone fireplace, cold now, stood against one wall, and on the opposite wall was a dresser beside a walk-in closet. It was perfect. Just like the rest of this house.

And right now, all it was lacking was Dave.

A knock on her door startled her out of her thoughts. She opened the door, looked up at Dave and knew that somehow this was meant to be. She wasn't going to question it. She was just going to *live*.

"You look like you're silently arguing with yourself," he said, his voice a low rumble of sound that seemed to reverberate in the big room.

"Nope," she said, shaking her head. "No arguing."

"No second-guessing?"

"No."

"No changing your mind?"

"No."

"Thank God." He stepped into the room and used one bare foot to kick the door shut behind him. "If you had changed your mind…"

"What?" she asked, excitement jolting to life inside her. "What would you have done?"

"Left," he admitted, then added, "and would have sat in my room, moaning in pain."

"That would have been a shame."

"Tell me about it," he said with a grin as he closed in on her. "You've been making me crazy, Mia."

"I have?" Oh, that was lovely to hear. She hadn't known she was capable of driving a man crazy.

"Oh, yeah." His gaze swept up and down her body and then met her eyes. "What's under the robe?"

"Me." She lifted her hands to the belt at her waist, but he stopped her.

"Let me."

She stood perfectly still while he untied the belt and pushed her robe open. The cool air in the room brushed her skin, raising goose bumps that were dissolved in the heat of Dave's touch.

His hands smoothed over her hips and up to cup her breasts. She swayed, but kept her eyes open, determined to see him, to experience every moment of this time with him.

He'd taken a shower, too, before coming to her. His dark blond hair was still damp. He wore a black T-shirt, jeans and he was barefoot. He looked sexier than she'd ever seen him and that was saying something.

He bent to kiss her and she moved into him, relishing the buzz of sensation as his mouth met hers. Once, twice and then he straightened up, looking down at her again. "Gotta have you, Mia."

"Yes, Dave." She reached up, wound her arms around his neck and whooshed out a surprised gasp when he scooped her up into his arms.

She laughed, delighted. It was all so romantic, she could hardly believe it was happening to her.

He took a step and stopped. "I surprised you," he said, grinning.

"You did."

"I like your smile."

She liked a lot about him. Staring into his eyes, Mia knew she should call a halt to this and knew just as well that she wouldn't. Sighing, she said, "Oh, this is really going to complicate things."

Dave shook his head. "Doesn't have to."

"Of course it does. Sex always complicates things."

"Complications aren't necessarily a bad thing."

"I hope you're right."

His grin widened briefly. "I'm always right."

He laid her down on the bed and she pushed herself up onto her elbows to watch as Dave stripped out of his clothes. In seconds, he was on the bed with her, gathering her up in his arms and rolling them across the mattress until she was breathless. Legs tangled, hands explored, mouths tasted, teased. Breath came fast and short and whispered moans and murmurs filled the room.

Mia arched into him when his mouth closed over her nipple. Lips, tongue and teeth worked her already sensitive skin until she was twisting and writhing beneath him, chasing the feeling that was growing inside her.

Mia had never felt like this. Never even come close. Dave was stroking her, dipping his fingers into her heat, touching her inside and out. And with every caress the fire engulfing her grew brighter, hotter. Her hips lifted into his hand, as she instinctively moved toward the release waiting for her.

"I've wanted to touch you like this for days," Dave murmured, then closed his mouth around one of her nipples.

"Oh…" She held his head to her breast and her eyes closed with the sheer bliss of the moment.

"I love the little sighs and moans you make," he said, lifting his head to look down into her eyes. "I love the way you feel. I love the scent of you."

Love. Love.

But not the Big L. A corner of her mind realized that and made sure she didn't cling to any false hopes. He didn't *love* her. He loved what they were *doing*. And so did she. *Don't think,* she ordered her mind and deliberately turned off everything but the sensations cresting inside her.

Again and again, he stroked, delved, caressed and nibbled. Foreplay became forever-play. She wanted him inside her and he kept making her wait. He was pushing her so high, so fast, she could hardly breathe with the wanting.

No one had ever touched her like this. No one had ever made her *feel* so much. He kissed her, using his tongue to steal the last of her breath. Mia didn't care. At that moment, all she cared about was finally, finally reaching the climax he was promising her with every stroke of his fingers.

When he broke the kiss and she reached for him, he grinned. "Hold that thought."

Then he eased off the bed, grabbed up his jeans from the floor and reached into one of the pockets. He tossed a handful of condoms onto the bedside table, then opened one of the foil packets.

A buzz of expectation sped through Mia as she shot a glance at the condoms, then at Dave. "Planning a long night?"

"Good to be prepared," he countered, and sheathed himself before joining her on the bed. "Now that I've got you where I want you, I may not let you go again."

"Who says I'm going to let *you* go?" Mia teased.

He grinned at her again. "That's what I like to hear." He dropped a kiss at the base of her throat. "You're so warm."

"Getting warmer every second," she said.

Smiling, he parted her thighs and knelt between them, pausing long enough to slide the tip of one finger along her folds, making her shiver.

She planted her feet on the bed and lifted her hips into his touch. Licking her lips, she murmured, "Please, Dave. No more waiting."

"No more waiting," he agreed and entered her in one long stroke.

Mia gasped, looked up into his eyes and sighed as she reveled in the sensation of him filling her. He was part of her. His body and hers locked together. She wrapped her arms around his neck and didn't take her gaze from his as he moved within her. Over and over again, he rocked his hips against hers, setting a rhythm that she eagerly matched. They moved as one, their bodies each straining toward a shattering climax.

Their sighs and groans filled the room like music. Sunlight speared through the windows and spotlighted them on the wide bed as they came together in a need that swamped everything else.

Mia held on to him as tension gripped her, coiling tighter and tighter. She moved with him, met him stroke for stroke. She slid her hands up and down his back and felt his muscles bunch.

This moment was all. Nothing beyond this room—this time—mattered.

She stared into his fog-gray eyes and watched her own reflection there as her body erupted. Mia called out his name and clung desperately to him as a shock wave thundered through her.

She was still trembling when Dave reached the same peak she had. And together, they slid down the other side into completion.

Eight

Dave was shaken, but damn if he'd admit it—even to himself.

Lying there on Mia's bed, with her curled up to his side, he stared at the ceiling and tried to understand just what the hell had happened.

He'd put her in this guest room on purpose. So she'd be close enough to make seduction that much easier. Problem was, *he* was the one who had been seduced. And that hadn't been part of the plan at all.

"That was so good," Mia murmured, her warm breath brushing across his chest.

"Yeah, it was." Better than good, he thought,

frowning a little as his brain began to click again now that the burn in his body had eased some. He'd figured from the beginning that getting Mia naked would take care of the desire that pumped through him every time he was near her. Instead, his body was stirring already at the feel of her hand stroking slowly across his chest.

Until today, he hadn't had a woman in more than six months. Just hadn't had the time or the inclination. Now it made sense, he thought. He'd needed a woman *badly,* so it was no wonder he'd been so frantic to get his hands on Mia.

The question was, why had the sex been so off-the-charts great? His mind was sluggish but still trying to find a way to save his ass. He'd spent more time with Mia than he had with any of the other women in his life. He *knew* her—had seen her at Alex's house. Talked with her in town. It was a connection that he'd always avoided with women before now, so of course the sex would be more…personal. More… Hell. Just *more.*

"I wonder if Delores has any chocolate cake left?" she murmured.

Dave laughed and looked down at her. Here

he was, thinking about taking another bite out of her and she had already moved on to chocolate. Humbling to know your woman was more interested in your housekeeper's home-baked desserts than she was in taking another ride.

Changing her mind about *that* was just the kind of challenge Dave liked best.

He went up on one elbow and looked down at her. "Chocolate cake's got nothing on what I'm about to give you."

"Really?" She lifted one hand to stroke her fingers along his chest.

Dave hissed in a breath. "Oh, yeah. When I'm done, you won't even remember what chocolate *is*."

As he slid down along her body, he felt her shiver and heard her whisper, "I can't wait..."

A few days later, Dave sipped his coffee and looked out the diner's window at the town of Royal, going about its day. He was tired. Hadn't been getting much sleep lately. He smiled to himself. Hell, once he and Mia had gotten started, there'd been no stopping either of them.

After their first night together, Mia had moved her things into the master bedroom and, Dave had to say, he was liking having her there. Strange because until Mia, he had never spent the night with a woman. It had always been get some, get gone. Easy. Uncomplicated. No expectations. No strings.

There weren't supposed to be strings now, either. But sometimes, Dave could swear he felt silky threads wrapping themselves around him, and he wasn't sure how to slip out of the knot that would only get tighter. Mia had been right, he told himself.

Sex had complicated the situation.

But he couldn't regret it. Hell, he'd have to be crazy to do that.

In fact, the only thing he was regretting was the fact that he had to leave her alone for a few days. Tonight, Dave was riding out with some of the ranch hands to where the herd was being held. The vet had already been out to inoculate the yearling calves and check out the rest of the cattle. He'd already taken care of the new beef that had arrived; now it was time for his regular herd to be checked over. Rather than ride in and out to the ranch, Dave and his employees would be camping out.

So he'd come to Royal to ask Nathan Battle to keep an eye on the ranch while Dave was gone. Not that he was worried about reporters getting to Mia. He was leaving enough of the ranch hands behind to see to her safety. But it never hurt to have a backup plan.

The Royal Diner was, as always, a morning hub of activity. He heard Amanda and Pam laughing at something, and the buzz of conversation from the other customers rose and fell like waves. Sunlight slanted through the windows, and outside an impatient driver hit the car horn.

From the corner of his eye, he saw someone approach, and expecting it to be Nathan, Dave turned his head and smiled a welcome. That smile froze in place when a lovely woman slid into the booth seat opposite him.

"Good morning," she said, shaking her hair back from her face and holding one hand out to him. "Remember me? I'm Bailey Collins. I work for the state investigator's office."

Dave shook her hand and released her. “I remember. We’ve ‘talked’ before.”

He studied her for a second or two. She had shoulder-length dark brown hair with reddish highlights. Her chocolate-colored eyes were locked with his as if daring him to look away. If she was waiting for him to cower, she had a long wait coming.

His good mood drained away as if it had never been. Dave had already talked to cops and private investigators about Alex’s disappearance and nothing had changed. He still knew nothing. Couldn’t help in their search. Didn’t have a clue what had happened to the man and was fast coming to the point where he didn’t care, either. Sure, if Dave had a choice in it, he’d like to see Alex come back safely. But more than that, he’d like to see people leaving *him* the hell alone.

“What do you want?” he asked, though he already knew the answer to that question.

She gave him a wide smile and shook her head. “Well, aren’t you charming?”

“I didn’t realize charm would make a difference with you.”

"It wouldn't," she admitted with a shrug.

"There you go, then." He wasn't going to play a game. Pretend to be understanding about all of this when his patience was long since shot to hell. So she could say her piece and get out of his life.

"All right," she said, "we're on the same page. I'm here in Royal to do my job, not make friends. I realize we've already spoken and that you're probably tired of answering questions, but I promise you, this will go much easier for both of us if you cooperate."

"Heard that before," he muttered.

She gave him a smile. "Look, why don't you tell me everything you know about Alex Santiago's disappearance."

"I'm sure you've read all the reports. I've told you already what I know and I can tell you now I haven't remembered anything new," he said, reaching for patience and just managing to grab hold of the tail end of it. "I've discussed it all with Nathan. With the feds. With you."

"And now," she said simply, "with *me* again."

Amanda walked up to the table, carrying a coffeepot. She looked from Dave to Bailey and back again. “More coffee?”

“Sure, thanks,” Dave said.

“Me, too. Thanks.” Bailey pushed the extra cup toward Amanda.

Once the cups were filled, Amanda gave Dave’s shoulder a pat in solidarity, then moved off again.

“You’ve got friends in town.”

“Guess I do,” he said, nodding. Funny, he’d never really thought about it before, but in the years that he’d been in Royal, he *had* made some good friends. He was grateful for them. Especially now.

Bailey doctored her perfectly good black coffee with cream and sugar, took a sip and said, “Why don’t you tell me one more time what you know about Alex’s disappearance.”

“It won’t take long,” Dave assured her. He launched into the story he’d already told too many times to count, and when he was finished, Bailey just looked at him for a long minute or two. They probably taught that move in investigator school. How to Make Potential Suspects Squirm 101.

But Dave had played with the big boys for a lot of years. He'd made deals, negotiated contracts and the one thing he'd learned had been "he who speaks first loses power." So he kept his mouth shut and waited her out.

It didn't take much longer.

"All right, thank you. I appreciate your time," she said and scooted out of the booth.

"That's it?" he asked, hardly daring to believe she wasn't going to pepper him with even more questions.

"You were expecting rubber hoses?" Her smile was friendly, but her eyes were still too sharp for comfort. "Oh. Just one more thing. I hear you're engaged to Alex's housekeeper Mia Hughes."

Dave went stone still. "And?"

"Nothing." She shrugged a little too casually. "It was sudden though, wasn't it?"

"I suppose. Is there a problem?"

She paused for a moment as if considering her answer before finally saying, "No. Look, I happen to agree with Sheriff Battle. You're not a suspect. But I have to talk to everyone who knew Alex. I'm hoping that someone knows something they don't even realize they know."

Nodding, Dave said, "Okay, I get that."

"Good." She stood up and bumped into Nathan Battle as he walked up to the booth. "Sorry, Sheriff, didn't see you there."

"It's okay." Nathan glanced at Dave, then looked at Bailey. "Am I interrupting?"

"No," she said with a last glance at Dave. "We're done here. Again, thanks for your time, Mr. Firestone."

When she walked away, Nathan took her seat, signaled to his wife, Amanda, for a cup of coffee then asked, "So what was that about?"

"The usual." Dave watched Bailey leave the diner and shook his head ruefully. "That was me, being officially ruled out by everyone."

"About time," Nathan said, wrapping one arm around his wife's expanding waist when she brought him coffee.

"Damn straight," Dave agreed and lifted his own coffee for a long, satisfying drink.

The next day, Mia was feeling Dave's absence. He'd ridden out early that morning with Mike Carter and several of the other ranch hands, and watching him ride off had torn at her. She hadn't even noticed over the past two weeks just how much she'd come to depend on having him around. They'd had a nice little routine going.

He worked outside and she studied in the library, preparing for her final exams. Yes, she still had time, but Mia wasn't taking chances with her future. They still managed to spend time with each other every day. They shared lunch, sometimes taking a picnic out to the lakeside. She helped him with the ranch ledgers and he'd showed her how to ride a horse. And one spectacular weekend, he'd arranged for his company plane to fly them to San Antonio. They'd had dinner on the River Walk and then went dancing. It had been the most romantic time in her life and it had ended all too soon. There had been warmth and laughter and an ease between them that she'd never felt with anyone else.

And now he was gone. Without him, the house felt bigger and far less warm. She could still smell him in the room they shared and caught herself listening for the sound of his boot heels on the floors.

But he would be gone at least two days, so Mia

was just going to have to deal with it. Actually, being without him would be good practice for when this month with him was over. When she moved back to her suite of rooms at Alex's house, she wouldn't be seeing Dave again. Wouldn't go to sleep in his arms or wake up to his kisses every morning. Her heart ached at the thought of that and she realized just how deeply she'd allowed herself to fall in the past couple of weeks.

Oh, Mia knew that she had been ripe for the kind of acceptance and belonging she'd found at the Royal Round Up. The ranch hands were wonderful. Delores, Dave's housekeeper, had practically adopted her. And the big house felt like home.

She'd hungered for *home* for so long, it was no wonder Mia had embraced what she'd found here. But it was so much more than that. She didn't want to think about it. Didn't want to even consider it. But the sad, hard truth was that she was falling in love with Dave. Oh, she knew that road led only to misery, but she didn't know what she could do about it now. And maybe she wouldn't change it even if she could. Yes, there would be pain coming her way, but the only way to avoid that pain was to not feel the way Dave made her feel. And she wouldn't give that up for anything.

Strange how everything, your whole world, could change so quickly. Just a few weeks ago, she'd been half convinced that Dave wasn't to be trusted. That he might have had something to do with Alex's disappearance.

Now she knew that the only thing he was guilty of was making her love him.

"Oh, this is not good," she muttered, closing the book on her lap.

She was curled up in a wide, leather chair in the library. There was a fire burning in the hearth and outside, gray clouds scuttled across the sky while a cold October wind rattled the trees and buffeted the windows.

The room was cozy and comforting but without Dave, it was empty.

She glanced at the sofa where they usually sat, wrapped up together, talking, laughing, *kissing.* A sigh slipped from her as she thought about how little time she had left with Dave. He'd set up a meeting with the owner of TexCat for next week.

Once he got the cattle deal he wanted, their time together would be over. And oh, how she would miss being here. Miss *him*.

When the phone beside her rang, Mia grabbed it, grateful for a reprieve from her own thoughts. "Hello?"

A woman's voice, quick and friendly. "Hello, may I speak to Dave?"

"No, he's out with the herd for a few days," Mia said, wondering who the woman was and why she wanted to speak to Dave. But in the next second she told herself that she had no right to wonder. She and Dave weren't a *real* couple, after all. But playing her role, she added, "I'm Mia, Dave's fiancée. Can I take a message?"

"His *fiancée?*" the woman repeated, her voice hitching a bit higher. "Isn't that *wonderful!* No, there's no message, thank you. I'll catch him another day. And, oh, congratulations!"

"Thank you," Mia said, but the woman had already hung up. Okay, she thought, setting the receiver back into its cradle, that was odd. But since the mystery woman seemed more excited than angry to hear Dave was engaged, Mia felt better about her. Sure, she didn't have the right to feel jealous, but that didn't stop the sharp sting of it.

Jealous. She had to get past that, because once their time together was over, Dave would be dating other women. Women who would come here, to this house. Be with him in his bed. Stare into those fog-gray eyes as his body claimed theirs.

And after a while, she thought dismally, Dave probably wouldn't even remember her.

By the time Dave got back to the house two days later, he was dusty, tired and damned crabby. Of course, he knew the reason for his bad mood.

It was Mia.

Or rather, the *lack* of Mia.

Spending those long nights out on the ranch used to be something he looked forward to. Getting away from the house, from the business side of things and getting back to the heart of ranching. Working the cattle, sleeping under the stars with nothing but a few cowboys and the crackle of a campfire for company. It kept him connected to his land and to the men who worked for him.

Now, thoughts of Mia, hunger for Mia, had ruined the whole damn experience for him. What the hell did that make him? What had happened when he wasn't looking? She was slipping under his skin. Getting to him in ways that he hadn't thought possible. Her laugh. Her scent. The feel of her long, supple fingers sliding over his body.

Everything about the woman was more than he'd expected. Who would have thought that a shy, quiet housekeeper would be so multilayered? So easy to talk to? Hell, she even liked playing video games and had damn near kicked his ass at one of his favorites.

She was only in his life temporarily. Their bargain was a business deal, that was all. Didn't matter if he had a good time with her. Didn't matter that he wanted her more than his next breath. When the deal was over, they'd go their separate ways. That was the point of a signed contract, he reminded himself. Rules were laid out, plain and simple, so there were no mistakes and no recriminations. If he wanted to keep the relationship with Mia going after the terms of the contract had played out—then that left him open to all sorts of trouble. He'd learned long ago that the only way to have a woman in his life was to keep it simple. Hence, the rules. Without them... Even wanting Mia as he did, he didn't think he could continue to see her when this was over. It would get...complicated.

Promises made were too easily broken. He wouldn't set himself up for that kind of misery. Better to have the "rules" laid out in black and white.

Yeah, the deal had become a little more than he had planned. After all, he'd expected that one night of sex with Mia would ease the craving for her. Instead, it had only grown until she was all he could think about. So yeah, a flaw or two in the plan.

But he'd find a way to get his equilibrium back. And when he did, he'd discover a way to keep Mia at a distance even while he was inside her.

Nodding, he told himself to get right on that.

But not tonight.

Tonight, he wanted a shower, and then Mia.

He opened the front door and stepped into the golden lamplight of home. Then he tore his hat off and tossed it onto a nearby chair. "Mia! I'm home!"

His gaze scanned the foyer, the wide, curving staircase and the hallway beyond. Where the hell was she? Then he heard it. Quick, light footsteps. He grinned, turned in anticipation and felt the air *whoosh* from his lungs in surprise.

A short, trim woman with chin-length blond hair and fog-gray eyes threw herself at him with a delighted grin. Dave wrapped his arms around her, returned her bear hug and said, "Mom? What're you doing here?"

Behind his mother, at a slower pace, came Mia. Her gaze met his and he read the worry in her usually sparkling blue eyes. But before he could figure out what was going on, his mother started talking. And once Alice Firestone got going, there was no stopping her.

"I can't believe you didn't tell me about Mia," she was saying, and reached up to pat his cheek just a little harder than necessary. "You should have told me. I'd have come sooner."

He finally found his voice. "Sooner than what? How long have you been here, Mom?"

Alice patted her son's chest as she stepped back and beamed at first him, then Mia. "I called to talk to you and when Mia answered and told me the good news, I came right away!"

"She arrived later the same day you left," Mia said, flashing him a silent "don't say anything" signal with her eyes.

"Naturally, I had to rush out here and meet my new almost daughter," Alice was saying. "So I called Tobin and he sent his plane for me. I was here in just a couple of hours."

Tobin. Damn. Dave hadn't thought about explaining the situation to either his partner or his mother and now he was paying the price. His mom had been after him for so long to get married and give her grandchildren that she wasn't going to take it well when she found out the engagement wasn't real. Perfect. And God knew whom Tobin was telling the news to. Dave shot a look at Mia and could see that her thoughts were running along the same lines.

"Oh, and Tobin said to tell you that he and his wife are so excited for you. They're planning a trip here to meet Mia as soon as they get back from North Dakota."

Great, he thought. More explanations to come. That's perfect.

"David, Mia and I have had so much fun these past two days," his mother said. "She's just a delight! Did you know that she'd like to have four children? Oh," she said, waving a hand in the air, "of course you know. The two of you probably have names all picked out."

Four children? He fired a look at Mia and she shrugged helplessly, turning both palms up. Marriage. Kids. Hell, this was getting out of control fast.

"Just so you know, I'm okay with whatever names you choose. I'll just be so pleased to have grandchildren!" Alice gave him a wide smile. "This is so exciting, David."

Before he could speak, Alice turned to Mia. "You know, sweetie, I've been so worried about him. I hated to think of him living his life alone. And then there was the guilt of course, for not exactly providing a good example of a happy marriage—"

"Hardly your fault, Mom," Dave interrupted. Damned if he'd let her feel guilty because Dave's no-good father had walked out on them.

"That's nice of you to say, honey, but a parent worries about their child *always.*" She reached up and brushed his hair off his forehead. "It doesn't matter if that child is an adult, the worry doesn't stop. Neither does the love. But you two will find that out for yourselves soon."

That noose he'd once felt locking around his throat was back again, tightening incrementally until Dave felt his breathing being choked off. Another glance at Mia and he read her expression easily. Misery and guilt. Well, hell, he knew how she felt, didn't he?

Damn, all he'd wanted was a shower and some hot, steamy sex with Mia. Now his brain was cluttered with his mother and imaginary children clambering all over his house. Talk about a mood killer.

Mia looked as if she wanted to crawl into a hole, and Dave understood. He should clear this up now, and he knew it. No point in waiting, because if he didn't cut his mother off at the pass, so to speak, she'd have a judge out at the ranch that weekend, performing a ceremony.

As if she read his thoughts, his mother said, "Mia and I were talking wedding plans, of course, *so* exciting. Mia insists you wouldn't want a large wedding…." She paused and watched him for confirmation.

"Yeah. I mean no, I don't."

"She knows you so well already," Alice said, eyes bright. "Isn't that lovely? So, we think it would be best if you hold the wedding right here on the ranch. There's plenty of room," she continued before he could say a word. "And Delores is full of wonderful ideas for a buffet menu. Mia and I can go shopping for her wedding dress—" She broke off and looked at Mia sheepishly.

"I'm sorry, honey. I'm just including myself, but of course if you don't want me to go with you…"

"It would be great, Alice," Mia said, her voice thick with emotion. "I'd love your opinion."

"Isn't that wonderful?" Alice turned back to Dave and gave him another hard hug before slapping one hand to her chest, overcome with emotion. "I always wanted a daughter, you know, and Mia and I already get along famously!"

Dave hugged his mom and regretted that he was going to have to burst her bubble. But that bubble would only get bigger and the hurt deeper, if he waited.

"Mom…" He looked over his mother's head to Mia who was shaking her head wildly and waving her hands. Narrowing her eyes, she glared at him and mouthed the word, *don't*.

Why the hell not? He scowled at her and she frowned right back, shaking her head again, even more firmly this time.

Fine, fine, he wouldn't say anything until he and Mia had had a chance to talk. Talking hadn't been on his agenda for tonight, but it looked like that was going to change.

Damn, he was too tired for all of this. He hugged his mother and let her go.

"Mom, I'm glad you're here, but after nearly three days on the range, I really need a shower."

His mother stepped back and sniffed delicately through her wrinkled nose. "I didn't want to say anything."

Wryly, he said, "Thanks."

Then his gaze shifted to Mia again and his mother noticed.

"Oh, you two must have a lot to 'talk' about." A smile flitted across her mouth. "Why don't you and Mia go on upstairs and I'll just head over to the guesthouse."

Dave was nodding. He was glad to see his mother, sure. But at the moment, he had other ideas on how to spend his time. At least he *had,* until this latest wrench had been tossed into his carefully laid-out strategy. Now he had the distinct feeling that Mia would want to talk before they did anything else.

When he just kept staring at Mia, his mother chuckled. "Okay, then, I'm going. You two enjoy your reunion and I'll see you both in the morning, all right?"

"That'd be good, Mom, thanks," Dave said, still staring at the woman who haunted his every thought. She chewed at her bottom lip and the action tugged at something inside him. Hell, maybe talking could wait after all.

He hardly noticed when his mother left until

the front door closed behind her. In the silence, he and Mia stared at each other for a long minute. Then she rushed at him and he opened his arms to her.

Holding on to her tightly, Dave buried his face in the curve of her neck and lifted her clean off the floor. Mia wrapped her legs around his waist, then pulled back and looked at him. "I really missed you."

Danger signs fluttered to life inside him, but it was way too late to pay attention to them. "Yeah," he admitted. "Me, too. And *damn* you smell good."

She gave him a smile and shook her hair back from her face. "I'm sorry you got blindsided by your mom, but I didn't know how to tell you she was here. I tried reaching you by cell, but…"

"It's okay," he said. "Not much coverage at the far corners of the ranch. Gotta get a satellite phone. I'm guessing her showing up out of the blue was a bigger surprise for you than for me anyway."

"You could say that." Her arms were linked around his neck, her ankles crossed at the small of his back. "She's so great, Dave. You're really lucky to have her."

"Yeah, but this is kind of a mess."

"More than you know," she said and unwound her legs from his waist to drop to the floor. Her eyes were shadowed and he knew she was feeling badly about deceiving his mother. Well, hell, so was he.

"She brought me a present."

Warily, he asked, "What?"

"I'll show you," she said on a sigh. "It's upstairs in your room."

"Just where I wanted to go, anyway." He dropped one arm around her shoulder and, pulling her in close to his side, headed for the staircase.

He didn't want to think about the fact that being with Mia made him feel…complete. Didn't want to acknowledge that the cold, hard spots inside him had been eased into warmth just by seeing her.

Because once he acknowledged any of that, there would be no going back.

Nine

Dave's room held more oversized furniture, just like the rest of the house. The bed was massive. A light oak four-poster was positioned against one wall. A flat-screen TV hung on the wall opposite and a bank of windows, drapes open to the night, took up another wall. There were scatter rugs in dark colors spread across the gleaming wood floor, a fireplace crackling with heat and two comfy chairs pulled up in front of the carefully laid blaze.

When Mia had first moved her things into this room, she'd felt a little awkward, out of place. Now it was cozy, filled with amazing memories of nights spent in Dave's arms and the promise of more to come.

He stood in the middle of the room and stripped out of his shirt. Tossing her a quick look, he said, "I'm going to jump into the shower, then we'll talk."

"Okay." Was it cowardly to prefer to put off the conversation she knew they had to have? If it was, she was fine with it. A few more minutes to gather her thoughts couldn't be a bad idea.

She heard the water when he turned it on and instantly pictured him in the shower. His long, rangy body covered in soap suds, hot water streaming across the hard planes and lines of the muscles carved into his skin by years of physical work. She pictured him tipping his head back under the rain showerhead, letting the water stream through his hair and down his back.

Swallowing hard, Mia edged off the bed. She didn't want to think. She just *wanted.* Dave had been gone for days and she'd missed him. Missed his touch. His taste. His scent. She'd missed what he could do to her body and she knew that conversation could wait.

She didn't want to waste a moment of her time with Dave. She loved him and all too soon, she'd be living without him. That thought made her heart ache as she walked across the room. So she put it aside for now. There would be plenty of time later for sorrow, for misery. Right now, there was only love.

She slipped out of her clothes as she crossed the bedroom and was naked by the time she walked into the adjoining bath. It looked like a spa in here. As big as her own living room at Alex's place, the bath was done in shades of green and cream tiles. There was a giant Jacuzzi tub sitting below an arched window that offered a wide view of the front of the ranch. A double vanity stretched the length of one wall, and on the opposite side of the room was a shower that could comfortably hold six people. There was no door, and because the area was so huge, no water from either the overhead rain nozzle or the five side sprays could reach the floor.

Dave had his back to her as he washed his hair and for just a minute, Mia simply enjoyed the view. He had the best butt in the world. And the rest of him was just as good.

Quietly, she slipped into the shower behind him and the hot water sluiced across her skin as she wrapped her arms around his waist and pressed her breasts against his back.

He groaned, turned around and cupped her face in his palms. “This kind of surprise I could use every day,” he whispered and dipped his head to kiss her, hard and long and deep.

Her mind fuzzed out, but her body leaped to life. Every inch of her skin was buzzing. Her insides lit up like a fireworks factory on fire and the sensation of the water coursing over them only added to the sexual heat stirring between them.

“I decided I’d rather not talk right away,” she said when he came up for air.

“My kind of girl,” he murmured, smiling into her eyes.

Mia wished it was true. Wished that what they had was more than a signed contract and a promise to lie to an entire town. She wished that what they felt when they came together would be enough to *keep* them together when the month was over, but she couldn't fool herself. Couldn't hang on to false hope. Couldn't set herself up for more pain than was already headed her way.

So, instead, she told her suddenly active mind to go to sleep. She didn't need to think. She only needed to *feel*. For now, that would have to be enough.

Still smiling, Dave used the soap dispenser on the wall of the shower and pumped some of the clear green gel into the palm of his hand. Then, scrubbing his palms together, he worked up a lather before cupping her breasts and smoothing the luxurious soap over her skin.

Mia sighed and swayed unsteadily. His thumbs worked her nipples into hard peaks and a burning ache set up shop between her legs. She moved into him, and ran her hands up and down his back and over his butt. She grazed him lightly with her fingernails and heard him hiss in a ragged breath. She smiled, knowing that he was as wildly needy as she was.

"God, you feel good," he told her, bending to kiss the curve of her neck and trail his lips and teeth back up the column of her throat to her mouth. "Taste good, too."

She shivered as he turned her until her back was against the smooth, gleaming tiles.

"Bet you taste good all over," he whispered and slid down the length of her body, taking his time about it, kissing her, stroking her until Mia was a quivering mass of sensation, pinned to the wall.

"Dave…"

The hot water rose up in steam all around them, blossoming like fog in the big bathroom. Mia opened her eyes and looked down to where he knelt in front of her and she swallowed past the knot of need and anticipation clogging her throat.

Dave nudged her thighs apart with his fingertips, and still meeting her gaze, rubbed the core of her with the pad of his thumb. Electrical jolts shattered her and she gasped in response, instinctively widening her stance for him, silently inviting more of his attentions. Again and again, he stroked her until Mia was whimpering with need.

She reached for him blindly, threaded her fingers through his hair and said, "Dave, please. I can't…"

"Yeah, you can," he murmured, then leaned in and took her with his mouth. Lips, tongue, teeth all worked her already sensitized flesh. He licked and tasted and nibbled until Mia's nerve endings were strung so tightly she thought she might simply explode into millions of tiny, needy pieces.

She braced one hand on the shower wall and with the other, she cupped the back of Dave's head, holding him to her. Her hips rocked in the rhythm he set and her breath came in short, hard gasps. Tipping her head back against the shower wall, she opened her eyes, stared into the steamy fog and felt lost. As if she'd been swallowed by sensation. There was no up. No down. There was only Dave and what he was doing to her.

"Dave… Oh…my…" Every word was a victory. Every breath a triumph.

When he pushed her closer and closer to the edge of completion, Mia looked down at him, wanting to see it all. Wanting to have this picture in her mind. So when she remembered this time with him she'd have something specific to torture herself with.

Then his tongue did a slow swirl over one

particular spot and the moment ended with Mia shouting his name as her body splintered all around him.

She couldn't stand, so Dave lowered her to the long, wide seat carved into the wall of the shower itself. Then he turned, adjusted a few of the shower jets, aiming them directly at the bench where Mia lay sensually sprawled.

"We're not done, you know," he said.

She fixed her eyes on him and gave him a slow satisfied smile. "I'm so happy to hear that."

Damn, this was some kind of woman, he told himself as he leaned over her, bracing his hands on either side of her head. She was beautiful and sexy and always ready for him. She was a match for him in a lot of ways, and if he were a man looking for a permanent woman, Mia Hughes would be the one he'd chase down and hog-tie.

But he didn't do permanent because there was no such thing. People made promises to each other all the damn time and broke them just as often. He wouldn't be part of that. Wouldn't make a promise only to let it shatter. Wouldn't walk out on his responsibilities. And the one way to make sure that didn't happen was to avoid making those "forever" kind of promises in the first damn place.

That's why he insisted on contracts for even the most minor deals. Harder to break a signed promise.

So he would have Mia as often as he could. He would give her all he had.

For the time they had together.

Then it would end.

She reached up and pushed his wet hair back from his face. Frowning slightly, she asked, "What're you thinking? You look so…sad, all of a sudden."

"It's nothing," he lied, and lowered his head to hers for a kiss. "Nothing."

She didn't look convinced, but he'd change her mind about that. His body was hard and hot and so damn eager he had to force himself out of the shower long enough to cross to the top drawer in the vanity. He yanked out a condom, tore the package open then worked the sheath down over his straining erection.

When he turned back to the shower, he saw that she was waiting, gaze fixed on him, and it wasn't worry he saw in her eyes now, it was need. Fresh. Raw. Powerful. He'd never been with a woman so in tune with his own desires. Mia was more than a match for him in so many damn ways he couldn't even count them all. But at the moment, it was their identical cravings that pulled at him.

He went back to her, and as the shower jets pummeled at their bodies, he levered himself over her and pushed himself into her depths.

Like every time with Mia, that first slide into her heat was a welcome into heaven. He felt surrounded by her, his body cradled within hers. She wrapped her arms around his neck, pulled his face down for a kiss, and he let himself drown in her. The heat of her. The sexual draw between them was overpowering, all consuming. And yet it wasn't just sex that simmered between them.

It was the connection he still feared and couldn't trust.

He moved inside her, pushing them both toward the climax he knew would crush him. Dave felt her shiver. Felt the first of the tremulous quakes racking her body and when she surrendered to them, he went with her. Giving himself up to what he had only found with Mia. The completion. The rush of pleasure, excitement and peace that existed only when he was in her arms.

A half hour later, they were dried off and in his bedroom. As she took a pair of jeans from a dresser drawer and tugged them on, he asked, "Sure you wouldn't rather just wrap up in robes? Be easier than getting out of all these clothes again later."

She whipped her hair back from her face and gave him a wicked smile that set his insides on fire. "A few clothes won't slow you down. Think of it as a challenge. Plus, I'm not cooking naked and I'm hungry."

He laughed. "Of course you are."

"Besides," she said as she tugged a long-sleeved, dark red sweater on over her head, "we still have to talk."

"Right." He grabbed a pair of his own jeans and pulled them on. He didn't bother with underwear, since his plan was to get her naked again as soon as he'd fed her. "Can't forget the talk. So. Before we head to the kitchen, you want to show me what my mom brought for you?"

She pointed. "It's in that box by the fire."

He spotted it on the table between the two armchairs. Barefoot and shirtless, he walked over and pulled the lid off. Beneath a layer of tissue paper was a white, lacy baby dress slightly yellowed from age. "What the—"

"It was your christening gown."

"Gown?" He turned around and stared at her, horrified. "I wore a dress?"

Mia laughed shortly and shook her head. "*That's* what's bothering you about this?"

"Hell, yes. Boys don't wear dresses."

"Not a dress. A gown."

"Same damn thing if you ask me." He dropped the offending item back into the box and set the lid in place again. "Why would she bring it to—" He broke off, tipped his head back and stared at the ceiling. "Oh, crap."

"Exactly." Mia sat on the edge of the bed, her bare feet dangling inches above the floor. "She brought it to me so we could use it for our baby's christening."

Mia wants four children. He could hear the glee in his mother's voice still. Four kids. And here's the dress they get to wear, poor things. Kids weren't in his plans, Dave reminded himself sternly even while a weird feeling crept over him. His mind provided an image to match that weird feeling and suddenly he had the mental picture of Mia, pregnant with his child. Even through the wave of terror the image projected, he could admit to himself that she looked lovely pregnant.

But there weren't going to be any babies.

He gave the closed box another glare and rubbed at the ache in the center of his chest. "This has gotten out of hand."

"I know."

Fixing his gaze on hers, he said, "You should have let me tell her the truth."

"I couldn't. She was so happy, Dave. So excited. So pleased for you and happy for *us*." Shaking her head, Mia sighed. "Alice has spent the past two days telling me all about you, showing me pictures of you as a child. She's…" Mia shrugged helplessly again. "I just couldn't tell her. And I couldn't let you, either."

"Mia, she's got to know." He wasn't looking forward to breaking that news, but he knew it had to be done.

Her voice was soft, but there was steel in her words when she said, "Please don't make me a liar to your mother."

"What? You're not a liar."

"Of course I am," she argued miserably. "While she was going on and on about how happy she was to have me for a daughter all I did was sit there, *basking* in it. She thinks we're really engaged and I *let* her think it. That makes me a liar and I can't stand the thought of her knowing."

"Mia..." He headed across the room to her, drawn to the slump of her shoulders and the distress in her voice.

She scooted off the bed and wrapped her arms around her middle in a classic self-protection stance. "I just don't want her to think badly of me, okay?" Looking up at him, she tried to explain. "I never had a mother, you know? I mean, she died when I was a baby and I always wondered what it would have been like if she had lived." She was talking faster now, as if words were gathering in the back of her throat waiting for their chance to be spoken. "How different would our lives have been? Having a mom teach you to cook. Going shopping for prom dresses. All the little things that I missed. I can't help but wonder what it would have been like to experience it all."

She took a deep breath and blew it out again. "I know how dumb that all sounds, but I swear, Dave, when Alice was talking to me and being so nice, I just…couldn't give that up by announcing that what you and I have is just role-playing. I couldn't do it."

He laid both hands on her shoulders and stared down into her eyes. "I get it," he said. "And trust me when I say I know how hard it is to get a word in edgewise when Alice Firestone is on a roll. She's like this gentle, sweet-natured steamroller. There's just no stopping her, so in your defense, she probably wouldn't have given you a chance to confess even if you'd wanted to."

Mia smiled up at him. "Steamroller, huh? She's a sweetie and you're lucky to have her."

"I know it," he said, "but she's flattened me a few times, too."

"Did you deserve it?"

"Probably," he admitted.

"Like I deserve it now," she muttered. Shaking her head, Mia shoved both hands through her hair, then let her hands drop to her sides. "But I'm asking you not to say anything to her, Dave. She's so nice and she loves you so much and she's so excited.... I'm a terrible person."

He chuckled and was rewarded with a frosty glare. "No, you're not. You're the exact opposite because you're worried about my mom's feelings in this."

"Yeah. I don't want her to think I'm a liar." Her head hit his chest. "Just don't tell her, all right? The month is almost up. You've got the meeting with TexCat arranged for next week. So just wait. When the deal is done, we'll break up as planned, and then she'll never have to know the real reason behind any of this. And she won't hate me."

She tipped her head back to look up at him. "I really don't want her to hate me, Dave."

In that moment, he would have given her anything, promised her whatever she wanted. Her blue eyes were drenched with emotion and the subtle sheen of tears she refused to let fall. She hadn't asked him for a thing since this whole bargain had started, so this request seemed reasonable. Besides, he was in no hurry to tell his mother her dreams of grandchildren weren't going to happen.

"Okay," he said, wrapping his arms around her. "We won't say anything until we have to."

She snaked her arms around his waist and held on. "Thanks."

"Sure." He kissed the top of her head. "Still hungry?"

"Am I breathing?"

Dave laughed, released her and gave her bottom a swift swat.

"Hey!" She grinned at him. "What was that for?"

"I just couldn't resist that cute little butt of yours, I guess."

"Maybe you could not resist me again after we eat?"

He grabbed a shirt, yanked it on and snatched her hand, tugging her out and down the hall to the stairs. "This is going to be the fastest meal in history."

Her laughter bubbled out around them and just for a second, Dave didn't worry about how happy Mia made him.

Mia reheated the stew Delores had made earlier and Dave managed to throw together some garlic bread. It was…*cozy,* being alone with her in the huge kitchen. Just the two of them, with the night outside the wide bay windows and lamplight casting a soft glow over the room. That ache in his chest was back, but Dave ignored it.

After they'd eaten, Mia put together a plate filled with cake and cookies for Dave to take to his mother in the guesthouse.

"She's probably getting ready for bed," he argued, since he'd rather take Mia back to their bedroom than take a walk.

"She's not ninety, Dave," Mia said with a laugh. "And she left before she got any of the cake."

Mia was polishing off a slice of Delores's famous mocha fudge cake as Dave picked up the plate with a resigned sigh. "I'll be right back."

Mia smiled at him and licked her fork lovingly. "Take your time…."

He watched her tongue make short work of the frosting on that fork and could only mutter, "Five minutes, tops."

Outside, it was cold, but Texas cold—so his bare feet on the flagstones didn't bother him a bit. He glanced around the ranch yard as he walked silently through the darkness. Dave noted lights on in the houses set aside for the ranch hands and frowned when he noticed the foreman's house was dark. Well, hell, on the ride home, all Mike had talked about was taking a shower and going to bed. Guess he meant it.

Shaking his head, Dave skirted the pool, walked past the line of Adirondack chairs and headed for the guesthouse. He'd built the damn place especially for his mother—he'd wanted her to live here, but to have her own space, too. Still, it had never been more than a way station for his mother, who refused to "be a wet blanket on her son's party." This time, though, he told himself, maybe he could get her to stay.

Once Mia was gone, the ranch was going to be…lonely. He frowned as that thought registered. Alone wasn't lonely, he insisted, but that argument was ringing false, even with him. He couldn't even imagine sleeping in his own bed without Mia beside him. Which told him that this whole situation was taking a turn he hadn't expected.

Dave was still frowning when he gave a perfunctory knock to his mother's door, then opened it. He stopped dead on the threshold and was pretty sure he'd been struck blind.

Mike Carter, wearing only a pair of white boxers, was *kissing* Dave's *mother.* Worse, she was kissing him back. And since when did mothers wear short nightgowns with spaghetti straps?

"What the hell?"

The couple broke apart at his shout and Mike whirled around to face Dave while at the same time shoving Alice behind him, standing in front of her like a human shield. "Dave—"

"What's going on here?" he demanded, then held up a hand. "Don't answer that!" He knew exactly what was going on and really didn't need any more details.

Dave set the covered plate down on the nearest table and took a step toward Mike. His friend. His foreman. The man he trusted more than anyone else in his life besides Tobin. "Mom, leave."

"I will not."

"Alice—" Mike said.

"Don't you start, either," Alice said and jumped out from behind Mike to face her furious son. "I will not run and hide as if I were a teenager being reprimanded by her parents. David Trahern Firestone, you just remember who the parent is here and who's the child."

"I'm no child," he ground out, hardly glancing at his mother. "And I want to know what the hell Mike is doing here like...*that*."

Alice bristled again. "You watch your tone, David, do you understand?"

"No!" he shouted, throwing both hands into

the air. "I *don't* understand. In fact, I think I'm having a stroke!"

"Oh, for heaven's sake!" Alice folded her arms across her chest and tapped the bare toes of one foot against the floor.

He couldn't think. Couldn't rationalize what he'd just seen, and then he heard himself babble, "What? How? When?"

"Dave, if we could talk…" Mike said, reaching for his jeans and pulling them on.

Fury was crouched at the base of his throat and betrayal was tightly wrapped around it like a fist. He could hardly talk, but he managed to say, "The only thing I'm saying to you is, you're fired."

His mother walked right up and slapped him. Dave just looked at her. She hadn't laid a hand on him since the year he was fifteen and took a ranch truck out for a joyride. "What was that for?"

"For being a boob," Alice told him, frowning. "You can't fire the man I love because you're embarrassed."

"I'm embarrassed?" He wasn't dealing with

hearing his mother say she loved a man. That was just too much for any son to have to take.

"Alice—"

Dave and his mother both said, "Butt out, Mike."

"Yes, you're embarrassed," she continued, looking at him now with less anger and more understanding. "Do you think I don't know the signs? You intruded here and now there's no way out but anger."

"Intruded." Okay, maybe he had, but in his defense, he hadn't expected to find his mother with— Don't go there.

"Honey," she said, "I'm a grown woman, and now that you yourself have found someone to love, I'm sure you can understand—"

Hysterical deafness set in. It was the only answer. Dave saw his mother's mouth moving, but he couldn't hear her over the roaring in his own ears. Mike and his mother? How long had that been going on? And what was he supposed to do about it? What *could* he do about it? Scrubbing both hands over his face, he took a breath and muttered, "Mom, stop. I beg you."

"Huh." She sniffed and picked up the plate of cake and cookies. "Oh, these look wonderful. Thank Mia for me since I'm sure you didn't think of this."

How had he come out to be the bad guy here? Dave gave up trying to talk to his mother and instead focused on Mike, who was watching him with a steady stare. The older man's chin was high, his shoulders squared as if he were expecting a firing squad. Well, hell. Now Dave felt like an idiot.

They were all adults here and he had barged in without thinking. And he had to admit, if his mom was going to fall for a man, at least she'd picked a good one. Still, there were a few things that had to be said.

"I want to talk to you," he muttered and turned to go outside.

"I think—" Alice said.

"Alice, honey, it'll be all right." Mike kissed her forehead and walked outside.

Dave sighed as his mother warned, "If you fire him, I will personally make you sorry, David."

He blew out a breath, stepped into the cool

night and stopped opposite his foreman. Mike still looked pugnacious, as if he were ready for anything. So just because, Dave punched him.

One swing and his fist slammed into the other man's jaw. Mike's head snapped back and his eyes flashed with fury. But he didn't lift a finger to defend himself.

"I figure you had that one coming, seeing as it's your mother and all. But hit me again and I'll hit back."

"How long has this been going on?" Dave demanded.

"I've been in love with your mother for years," Mike admitted on a sigh. "She wanted to tell you but I wouldn't let her."

"Are you using her?"

Mike glared at him. "I might just hit you anyway. I love her. And now that you've got Mia in your life, I figure you can understand how that feels. If you can't, I'll leave the ranch. You won't have to fire me. But know this. I won't give Alice up."

Everybody figured now that he had Mia he could understand love. Well, they were wrong.

He didn't understand it, didn't trust it and didn't see that changing any time soon. Need was different. It was clean. Uncomplicated.

Dave's mind was racing. Everything was changing around him so fast he could hardly keep up. His world used to be so neat and tidy. He'd had complete control over his universe and he couldn't figure out where it had all gone wrong.

"Oh, relax," Dave told his old friend. "You're not fired and I'm not hitting you again— Unless," he added quickly, "you make her cry. Then all bets are off."

"Agreed," Mike said.

"Sorry I barged in," Dave said. "*Really* sorry. There are just some things sons shouldn't see."

Mike snorted a laugh. "Guess that's so. If it makes you feel better, I've about convinced Alice to move into the guesthouse permanently."

"Yeah?" He smiled, then frowned and jabbed a finger at his foreman. "If you're thinking you're living there with her—not unless you're married."

Mike grinned. "My pleasure. Now…I've got a reunion of my own to get back to."

Dave watched him go and shuddered. "No, some things a son should never even know about."

Back at the house, Mia watched as Dave stalked around the perimeter of the lamp-lit kitchen, talking more to himself than to her.

"I don't get it," he muttered. "Love? How the hell could she be in love? She loved my father and that didn't stop him from abandoning us."

"Mike's a good guy," she argued.

"Yeah," he agreed, never slowing his pace. "But that doesn't guarantee anything, either."

"There are no guarantees," Mia pointed out, turning in her seat to keep her gaze locked on him. He was shaking his head, muttering, and that frown carved into his features looked as if it was there to stay.

"That's the whole point," he told her. "Without a guarantee, why take the risk? Love is just a word. It doesn't *mean* anything."

"It means everything," she said softly and felt a hitch in her chest when he stopped pacing to stare at her.

She couldn't tell what he was thinking, and maybe that was just as well, she thought.

"No," he said quietly, "what you and I have is more. Desire is straightforward. Uncomplicated. It doesn't screw with your life and you don't get flattened when it ends."

Mia heard every word and felt them like a direct slap to the heart. He believed everything he was saying. She knew that. And she realized finally and at last that he would never allow himself to love her. Never risk his heart.

Which meant that though she was still here and with him, what they had was already over.

Ten

Thomas Buckley was an ass.

The owner of TexCat was short, balding and very well fed. His cheeks were red, his blue eyes were sharp and his ideas were straight out of the 1950s.

"A family man is a man to be trusted," Buckley was saying, smiling benevolently from behind his wide, ostentatious desk. "I always say if a man can't make a commitment to a woman, then he can't keep his word on a deal."

Dave had already sat through more than an hour of listening to the older man pontificate about morality and family values. It felt like a week. He could only imagine what Mia or his mother would say about Buckley's take on women being "the gentle sex, God bless 'em" and how they "don't understand men's business, but they keep our homes and raise our children and that's enough."

Seriously, Buckley was dancing on Dave's last nerve.

When he finally wound down, Dave asked, "So, we have a deal?"

"I've had my man go and check out your herd and he tells me it's some of the best beef he's seen in years." Buckley threaded his fingers together and laid them across his corpulent belly as he leaned back in his desk chair.

"Not surprised," Dave said quickly. "My ranch is completely organic. No feedlots, either. The land is managed so that the herd has free range and we don't take on more cattle than we can comfortably support."

Buckley nodded. "That was in the report, as well. And you say you're engaged to be married?"

Briefly, he gritted his teeth. "Yes. Mia's studying to be a school psychologist."

"Well, that'll be fine I'm sure, until your first child is born. Then she'll want to stay home."

If he gritted his teeth for much longer, Dave thought, he'd leave this office with nothing more than a mouth full of powder. "Plenty of time to think about that."

"You're right, you're right." Buckley sat up straight, held out his right hand and when Dave shook it, the older man smiled. "We've got a deal. Let's get the paperwork signed."

An hour later, Dave was back in Royal, glad to be back from Midland and the TexCat offices. He'd done it. His ranch's reputation was set now that he had that all-important deal. His plans for the future were looking good and the bargain he'd struck with Mia was now completed.

All that was left was to tell her the good news and end their faux engagement. Odd how that thought didn't fill him with pleasure. So instead of heading back to his own place, Dave drove into town to see Nathan Battle. He needed a friend to talk to.

"I don't see the problem." Nathan poured two cups of coffee and handed one to Dave. Carrying his own coffee, Nathan walked around his desk and propped his booted feet up on one corner.

The Royal jailhouse was small, but it boasted up-to-date equipment and a casual feel. Nathan had one deputy, and between the two men, the small town's citizens were taken care of.

"The problem is," Dave said, after a sip of the strong, hot coffee, "I don't need a fiancée anymore, but I don't want to end this with Mia, either."

"Ah." Nathan nodded sagely. "So, basically, you're screwed?"

"To sum it up, yeah."

"You don't have to end things, you know," Nathan mused.

Dave fired a hard look at his friend. "I've considered that…"

"And?"

"Don't know." He stood up, set his coffee on the edge of the desk and started pacing. The wood floors held plenty of scuff marks from generations of boots stomping across them, and the wide front window overlooked Main Street. Dave shoved his hands into his back pockets, stopped at the window and stared, not seeing the town beyond the glass.

His mind raced with more questions than answers. For the first time in years, Dave was unsure what move to make. All he knew was that he didn't want to lose Mia. Not yet, anyway.

Of course, he didn't plan to *keep* her in his life. They'd made a deal after all. Signed a contract. Their engagement would end and they'd each go back to their own lives.

But he wasn't ready for that.

"Stop thinking about what you should do and tell me what you *want* to do," Nathan suggested.

Dave glanced at him over his shoulder. "What I want is to go home and see Mia."

"So do that and forget about the rest for now."

"Just like that?"

"What's the hurry? You said yourself the deal you made with Mia goes to the end of the month."

"Or until I get the contract, whichever comes first."

"There's no saying you can't renegotiate, though, right?"

"True." Great sex must have clogged his brain.

Otherwise he would have thought of this solution himself. There was no reason he and Mia couldn't strike a new deal. They were good together. Maybe this was worth looking into.

"Give yourself some time to figure out what you want to do. The TCC's big Halloween party is in a few days. At least wait until after that."

He thought about it and realized that Nathan was right about something at least. Renegotiation could work. He wasn't ready to give Mia up.

"Dave, you don't have to have every answer to every question at all times."

He laughed and shoved one hand through his hair. "You know, until now, I always have."

"Things change," Nathan said with a shrug. "Trust me, no one knows that better than I do."

"Things are changing too damn much lately," Dave muttered.

Nathan chuckled. "Yeah, I heard about your mom and Mike Carter."

"Don't remind me," Dave said. It had been almost a week since the night he'd blundered into the middle of his mother's—whatever. He was almost used to the fact that his mom was in love. He wasn't used to Mike Carter living in the guesthouse with her.

Alice was happy like Dave hadn't seen since he was a kid, before his father left them. He was glad for his mom, but he couldn't understand how she could have faith again. Trust again, after how Dave's father had let her down. Abandoned them.

How did she let go of the past and risk taking another chance on love? Shaking his head, Dave told himself that Thomas Buckley had it all wrong.

Women were much stronger than men.

"Congratulations," Mia said and hoped she sounded more sincere than she felt.

"Thanks." Dave poured them each a glass of wine and handed one to her. They took their usual spots on the sofa in the library as he told her about the deal with TexCat.

She listened and tried to look happy for him, but inside she was a mess. Her heart felt twisted into a knot and breathing was so difficult, she didn't even sip at her wine, half-afraid she'd choke to death. That was it. It was done. She and Dave were over. The signed contract with TexCat signaled the end of their bargain.

Now she could move back to Alex's place and get on with her life. The only problem? She wasn't sure she *had* a life without Dave.

"I'd like you to stay," he said suddenly, grabbing her attention.

Mia's heart clenched. Her gaze locked on his. "What?"

He took her wine and set both glasses on the polished wood table in front of them before turning back to her. Dropping both hands on her shoulders, he pulled her in close, looked into her eyes and said, "I'd like you to stay—"

Hope roared to life inside her.

"—until the end of the month," he finished.

And hope drained away again, leaving her feeling surprisingly empty. He didn't want her forever. She'd been fooling herself thinking that maybe because *she* loved, that he did, too. Well, here was the eye-opener, the back-to-reality talk she'd been dreading for weeks.

"Why?"

"Why not?" he countered and gave her shoulders a squeeze.

Amazing, even though the heat of his hands was sliding through the fabric of her shirt to seep into her body, she still felt cold.

"Look, Mia," he said softly, "we've had a good time, right?"

A good time. She sighed. "Yes."

"So why let it end before either of us is ready?"

Because if she stayed much longer, she didn't know how she would leave at all. And she had to leave, she told herself firmly. She couldn't stay with a man who didn't love her. It would kill her by inches.

Shaking her head, she said, "I don't think that's a good idea."

"Why the hell not?"

She smiled. He really had a hard time when people didn't fall in with his plans. "Because we both have lives we have to get back to. I take my final exams soon and then I'll have to get busy looking for a job—"

"Royal School District is going to hire you," he said, brushing that concern aside.

"Maybe," she said. "But there's no guarantee. So I'll have to apply to school districts in Midland and Houston, too."

He scowled at her. "You didn't tell me."

No, she hadn't. Because she hadn't wanted to think about it herself. The thought of moving away from Royal made her heartsick. She hated the thought of leaving before Alex came back and she was really hoping that Royal would hire her. And if they didn't, maybe she'd end up looking for a job here in town until everything was back to normal. Leaving without having the mystery of Alex's disappearance settled seemed impossible.

Besides, she didn't want to move from Royal, the only home she'd ever known. If she did, that would mean she wouldn't even be able to catch the occasional glimpse of Dave around town. Maybe that would be better, but at the moment, she didn't think so.

"The point is," she said, trying not to think about moving, "our time together's over."

He was still frowning when he said, "At least stay through the TCC Halloween party. That's only a few days away."

"Why?" she asked, suddenly so tired she wanted to go lay down with a pillow over her head.

"Because I'm asking you to," he whispered.

He never asked, she told herself silently. He ordered. Or growled. Or dictated. But he was asking her, and as she looked into his fog-gray eyes, she knew she wasn't ready to leave. Not yet. "I'll stay."

Three days later, Mia stepped out of the ranch house in time to see her VW being towed away. She took an instinctive step or two to chase after it, even knowing there was no way she could catch it.

She glanced around the ranch yard, hoping to find someone to tell her she'd just had a hallucination. Instead, she saw Dave, standing beside a brand-new, shiny, luxury SUV.

For the past several days, he'd been…different. Ever since their talk in the library the night he'd gotten the deal with TexCat, things had changed between them. Oh, they were still together every night, but even their lovemaking had a different feel to it. Like a prolonged goodbye that was tearing Mia apart, piece by piece.

Now, as he watched her, she saw the same expression on his face that had been there the past few days. Not cold, exactly. But more…distant than she was used to. It was as if every time he saw her, he was letting go. She felt as though there were a giant clock inside her ticking off the minutes, and when that clock hit zero, there would be nothing left between her and Dave.

So instead of enjoying their last week together, they were each of them holding back, protecting themselves and their hearts. If she had any sense, she'd leave. But she just couldn't. Even though being here was painful, being away from Dave would be worse.

He walked toward her, every step long and determined. His features looked carved from granite and his gray eyes gave nothing away.

When he was close enough, she asked, "Who took my car? And *why?*"

"That's not a car," he countered. "It's a disaster waiting to happen. Just yesterday you got stuck on the side of the road coming home from Alex's."

"I just needed some gas." Fine, she probably needed a new gas gauge, too.

"No, you needed a new car and now you've got one." He pointed at the silver beauty.

"You did *not* buy me a car," she whispered.

"Yeah, I did. Deal with it." His voice was clipped, his eyes fierce, as if he was preparing for battle.

Well, he was going to get one. Dave Firestone was used to rolling over people to get his own way, but she wouldn't go down without a fight. Even though there was a part of her insisting that she just shut up and accept that pretty, brand-new, worry-free car.

"This wasn't part of our deal," she argued, silencing her internal voice.

"Yeah, well, I renegotiated it on my own." He grabbed her shoulders and yanked her in close. "You told me you've applied for jobs in Midland and Houston. You think I'm going to worry about you off somewhere alone in that crappy car? Not gonna happen." Shaking his head, he let her go and turned for the barn.

"This isn't over!" she called after him, even though she knew it was. Her car was gone. She shifted her gaze to the new beast shining in the sunlight.

Mia moved closer and did a slow walk around the simply gorgeous luxury SUV. She opened the driver's side door and looked inside. The interior was navy blue leather and the smell… She took a deep breath and sighed it out. Mia had never in her life owned a *new* car. All of her cars had been new to her, but considerably aged by the time she'd gotten hold of them.

She reached out one hand and smoothed her palm over the baby-soft leather seat, and for one long second, she experienced pure avarice. What would it be like, she wondered, to drive a car and not have to worry about the engine falling out? To not have to carry a case of oil with you everywhere you went? To turn the key and have the engine fire right up without the help of prayers and desperate pleas?

Frowning, Mia forced herself to step back and

close the door. Her hand might have lingered on the door handle, but who could blame her? It was beautiful. And extravagant and she absolutely couldn't keep it. She and Dave had a deal. A signed contract. And a new car wasn't part of it.

"Isn't that lovely?" Alice came up behind her and Mia turned to smile a welcome.

"It is."

"Yet you don't look happy with it."

"It's great, Alice," Mia told her with a sigh. "But I can't keep it."

"Why ever not?"

"It's complicated," Mia said, hoping the other woman would accept that and let it go.

"Mia, I know David can be impulsive. Heck, he bought me a new car just a few weeks ago and didn't bother to tell me about it beforehand."

"But you're his mom."

"And you're his fiancée." She laid one hand on Mia's forearm. "Did he surprise you with this? Are you angry that he didn't talk to you about it? Is it that you don't like the color?"

Mia laughed. Imagine saying no to a new car

because you didn't like the color. "No, the color's just right. And I like surprises…"

"Then why shouldn't he buy you a car?"

"Because we're not getting married," she blurted. Oh, God. The words had just jumped from her mouth before she had a chance to stop them. She slapped one hand to her mouth, but it was too late. The truth was out and now Alice would hate her and Dave would be furious that she'd told his mother.

"I know."

"What?"

Alice smiled, put her arm around Mia's shoulder and gave her a squeeze. "Honey, I know my son better than anyone. He doesn't go from 'never getting married' to 'I'm engaged' overnight. I knew something was up, I just didn't know what."

"Alice, I'm so sorry…" This wasn't fair. She was so nice. So understanding. So…mom-like. "I didn't want to lie to you, but I didn't want you to hate me and I asked Dave not to tell you, so it's not even all his fault. It's just so complicated."

Alice gave her another hug. "Good stories always are," she said and started walking toward the house. "Now, why don't we get some tea and some of Delores's cookies and you can tell me everything."

Too late to do anything else, Mia nodded, and allowed herself to be mothered for the very first time.

Over two pots of tea and enough cookies to make even Mia a little sick, she told Alice the whole story. When she finally wound down, she was spent. Tears still dampened her cheeks, but her breathing was easier than it had been since she'd started living a lie.

"You love my son, don't you?"

"Yes," Mia said, "but it doesn't matter."

"It's all that matters." Alice poured more tea for each of them and said, "David loves you, too."

Mia had to laugh. He wanted her, she knew that. Heck, they couldn't be in the same room together for more than five minutes without leaping at each other. But desire wasn't love and want wasn't need.

"You're wrong."

Alice shook her head. "There's a shiny new SUV parked out front that says different."

"The car?"

"It's more than a car, honey." Alice sat up, reached out and took Mia's hands in hers. "Remember, a few weeks ago, David had a new car delivered to my house."

"Yes, but you're his mother."

"And he loves me. Worries about me driving a car he doesn't think is safe."

"He hates my car," Mia murmured.

"So he replaced it with a much safer one. And if he didn't love you, why would your safety matter to him?"

"I don't know…." She'd like to believe that. But how could she?

"It's David's way, Mia," Alice was saying. "Ever since he was a child, he's had trouble with the word *love.* But that doesn't mean he doesn't *feel* it."

A tiny kernel of hope settled in the pit of her stomach, but Mia couldn't put too much faith in it. Because if she did and Alice was wrong, her heart would be crushed beyond repair.

Loud music pumped out of speakers. Orange and black streamers and balloons hung from the ceiling, drifting with the movements of the crowd. Dry ice near the punchbowl sent clouds of vapor into the air. Vampires danced with angels, zombies loitered near the buffet table and a princess stole a kiss from a troll.

All in all, the TCC costume party was a rousing success. The club wasn't just celebrating Halloween this year, but also the opening of the new day-care center. So much fuss had been made about the center over the past few months, it was a wonder anything had gotten done.

But Mia had already taken a tour of the new day-care center and she was impressed with the place. Glancing into the large, well-appointed room, she saw lots of tiny tables and chairs for the kids. Bookshelves were stocked with row after row of wonderful stories. There were cribs for infants and on one side of the room small easels were set up, ready for little artists to paint their masterpieces.

"Isn't it wonderful?" A woman's voice spoke up from right beside her and Mia jumped. She hadn't noticed anyone approach.

The woman was a few inches shorter than Mia,

with jaw-length blond hair and brown eyes that were sparkling with excitement.

"I'm sorry," she said. "I didn't mean to sneak up on you. But I saw you looking in at the day care and couldn't resist coming over." She held out one hand. "I'm Kiley Roberts, and I'll be running the center."

"Mia Hughes. It's nice to meet you." Mia shook her hand and said, "I was just thinking how impressive it is that the center has come together so nicely despite all the battles."

"Oh, I know." Kiley sighed a little. "I'm glad it's all settled and over. My little girl, Emmie, can't wait to start coming here."

"How old is she?"

"Two," Kiley said, "and she's the light of my life." She paused, spotted someone walking into the center and said, "Excuse me, I should go direct another tour."

Mia nodded as the woman moved off, practically dancing with excitement for the opening of the center. She envied Kiley Roberts, Mia realized. Kiley had a plan. A future stretched out ahead of her, and she had a child. A family.

Smiling wistfully, Mia turned away from the center, walked over to the open doorway into the main room and looked out over the gathered crowd. She spotted Dave across the room at the bar, standing beside Nathan Battle. The two men laughed at something and Mia's heart twisted in her chest. Dave looked wonderful as an Old West outlaw. Dressed almost entirely in black, he looked dangerous and sexy. A lethal combination, as Mia knew only too well.

As if he could feel her gaze on him, he turned, met her eyes and gave her the half smile that never failed to tug at her heart. God, how she would miss him.

He left Nathan, made his way over to her through the crowd and when he stopped directly in front of her, he said, "Did I mention that you make the most beautiful saloon girl I've ever seen?"

Her costume deliberately went along with his. Her dark blue satin dress was trimmed with black lace at the bodice and the hem of her full skirt. She wore fishnet stockings, black pumps and her upswept hair had blue feathers tucked into the mass.

"I think you might have said something along those lines," she said.

"It's worth repeating." He took her hand and led her toward the dance floor. "Dance with me, Mia."

She couldn't have resisted him even if she'd wanted to.

He pulled her into the circle of his arms and began to sway in time with the music. All around her, the citizens of Royal were celebrating. There was laughter and shouts and conversations pitched at a level to be heard over the music.

Mia laid her head on his chest and followed his lead around the dance floor. It was magical and sad and special all at once. She'd have loved for the music to spin on for years, keeping them here, locked together. But she knew that couldn't happen; all too soon, the night would end and, like Cinderella, her magic would be over.

"Marry me, Mia," he whispered.

And the whole world stopped.

Eleven

"What?"

Dave grinned. He'd caught her off guard. Good. Just how he wanted her. If she was off balance, she wouldn't be so eager to argue with him. He'd never met a more hardheaded woman.

"Marry me." Hell, even he couldn't believe he was serious. But the thought of losing Mia was driving him nuts.

She went limp in his arms and he took that as a good sign. The noise level inside the club was near deafening and to make his case he'd need to get where he could talk to her loud enough to be heard.

"You want to get married?"

"Absolutely," he told her, bending his head so he wouldn't have to shout and so that no one else could hear him. "I've thought it all out and it's the best solution to the situation."

The past few days had been crazed, him knowing that she would be leaving and not having a way to keep her there, short of tying her to his bed—which didn't sound like a bad plan to him at all.

But since that would be a temporary solution, he'd come up with something better. A marriage based not on love but logic.

She shook her head as if to clear it, then looked into his eyes and asked, "You love me?"

Something fisted tight around his heart, but Dave ignored it. This wasn't about something as ephemeral as *feelings.* This was about— Hell.

"Who said anything about love?" He frowned a little and danced them over to a corner of the floor where they would be more alone. When they were far enough away from the crowd, he backed her into a corner and stared down at her.

"I'm not talking about love. I'm talking about a contract."

"A what? You mean a prenup?"

"No." He smiled at her. "I mean a contract where we promise each other we'll stay together. No divorce. No leaving. And we both sign it."

"You're kidding, right?" She blinked up at him and he had the distinct impression he was losing her.

He couldn't lose her. That was the one thing he'd figured out over the past few days. The thought of her moving to Midland or Houston was enough to drive a spike through his heart. So, yeah, he could admit that he cared for her. A lot. But he wouldn't offer a promise that was too easily broken. Love was too iffy. Too…dangerous.

"A signed contract is better than some lame promise to love and cherish. It's a legal document," he insisted. "One you can count on."

"Dave…a contract isn't a guarantee against failure."

All around them, Royal was in party mode. The music continued to pump into the room and wild laughter and shouts rose up behind them. Dave had come here convinced that he'd found a way to keep Mia with him. Now, though, here in this darkened corner in the middle of a celebration, Dave felt as though he were losing a war.

"No, it's not. But it's a start. Running your life on emotion is asking for trouble," he told her flatly. "I know because I've seen it up close and personal. I want you with me, Mia. But I can't promise love."

She reached up, cupped his cheek in the palm of her hand and said, "And that's the only thing I want from you."

Her hand dropped from his face, but he caught it in his and dragged it back up, holding her there, feeling the heat of her even as he saw a chill creep into her eyes. He had to keep trying, though, because he'd never once given up on something he wanted.

"We're good together, Mia," he said and saw a flash of hurt dart across her eyes. "You know it. We've been happy this past month."

"Yes, we have," she said, pulling her hand free of his. "But it's not enough for me. Not anymore."

"Why *not?*"

"Because I love you, Dave." She took a deep breath, blew it out again and gave him a sad smile. "I didn't mean to, it just happened."

A quick flash of something bright and amazing shot through Dave in a split second before his brain kicked into gear and rejected the emotion. He'd learned long ago that "love" was just a word. He stiffened. Looking down into her face, he read the truth in her eyes and took an emotional step back. "Love wasn't part of the agreement."

"No," she said sadly, "it wasn't."

He glanced over her head at the crowd in the room behind them, away from her eyes, giving himself a chance to take a mental breath. To get a grip. It didn't help much. "I'm not interested in love, Mia. I told you that from the beginning."

"Yeah, you did." Mia shook her head so hard, one of the feathers in her hair came free and floated to the floor. "I should have listened. But I love you anyway."

He scraped one hand across the back of his neck, then looked into those eyes of hers again.

"Stop saying that," he muttered darkly. "People say that damn word so easily."

"I don't," she told him flatly. "I've never said 'I love you' to a man before. Ever."

He gritted his teeth. "Love wasn't part of our deal."

"And the deal is all-important?" she asked. "Rules? Contracts?"

"Without them, you've got nothing," he countered, his voice harsh and deep. "Love is a setup for the letdown, that's all. Throw that word out and you're supposed to forget common sense. You're supposed to believe—" he broke off and caught himself before saying "—you believe promises and one by one they're broken."

"What're you talking about?"

"Love," he snapped and wondered when this whole thing had gone to hell. "My mother believed. My father said he loved her. Us." He laughed shortly and heard the sharp, ragged edges of it. "Didn't stop him from leaving. Walking away, leaving Mom to survive however she could. We lost our home. We lost everything. I became the man of the house when he took off.

I was eleven. I stopped being a kid and watched my mother's world crumble around her. Because we believed in *love*."

"Dave…" She reached out to him but he stepped back. "That's awful and I'm so sorry…"

"Didn't ask for your pity."

"Sympathy, not pity," she corrected. "And your mom is in love again. Do you think Mike will break her heart?"

"He better damn well not."

Shaking her head, Mia said, "He won't. He's a good man and he loves her. Your mom is willing to take a chance again, so why can't you?"

God, it was hot in there. He felt like he couldn't breathe. He'd spilled his guts and she was picking them up and handing them to him. And Dave didn't have a damn answer for her. He didn't understand how his mother could trust again. Believe again. He only knew that he couldn't. He wanted Mia. Cared for her more than anyone he'd ever known. But if he used the word "love," he'd lose control.

"I won't give you promises, Mia," he told her,

gathering the threads of his control. "I'll give you a contract. My word. In writing."

"Without the promise, the contract means nothing, Dave. Don't you see that?"

"Why are you doing this?" he demanded, reaching for her, grabbing hold of her shoulders and dragging her close. "We had a deal. You weren't supposed to bring emotions into this."

She laughed a little, but it was a broken sound. "Pesky humans, you just can't trust them to keep their hearts out of things."

"Damn it, Mia, I don't want to lose you. We can still have something good together."

"No. But we could have had something *great*."

"You're wrong."

"Looks like I was wrong about a lot of things," she whispered. Slowly, she pulled the huge diamond ring from her finger and held it out to him. He stiffened, gritted his teeth against the unfamiliar swell of helplessness filling him and took the ring from her, closing his fingers over the cold, hard stone.

She walked past him then, without another word. He wanted to reach for her, pull her into his arms and never let go. But he knew it wouldn't do any good. She was already gone.

He'd lost.

Amanda and Nathan gave Mia a ride to Alex's house. Thankfully, her friends didn't ask any questions. The gate guard at Pine Valley let Mia into the house and when she was alone in what had once been her home, she gave in to the tears strangling her.

All the silly, foolish hope she'd been hanging on to for weeks dissolved in that flood of sorrow. By the following morning, Mia was still miserable, and looked every inch of it.

She forced herself to get up and on with her life, because even though her heart hurt and her eyes were still red and swollen from crying, she had to keep moving. If she surrendered to her misery, she'd never leave Alex's house again.

A glance out the front window let her know that Dave had had her new car delivered. Had he brought it himself and left without seeing her? Had he had one of the ranch hands deliver it instead so he wouldn't have to risk seeing her? Did it matter?

She looked at the shiny new car in the driveway and Alice's words came back to her. *He gave you a car because he loves you.* Mia would like to believe that, but unless he actually said the words, she couldn't.

Her purse and clothes were all in the SUV, carefully packed in her suitcases. She carted everything inside and once she'd unpacked, she realized that she had better go grocery shopping. Delores wasn't around to spoil her anymore. She was on her own again and she better get used to it.

In town, she stopped in at the diner to thank Amanda for the ride home and found the whole coffee shop buzzing. People seemed angry, confused, as they gathered in groups to talk. Mia took a seat at the counter and when Amanda poured her a cup of coffee, she asked, "What's going on?"

"You haven't heard yet? The whole town's talking about it. I got the story from Nathan, of course, and I just could hardly believe it."

Amanda bit her lip, shook her head and said, "It's the day-care center at the TCC."

Mia had a bad feeling about this. "What happened?"

"Someone broke in last night and vandalized it."

This wasn't the first time someone had tampered with the day-care center, Mia knew. But this sounded far worse than before.

"Oh, no! But it was so beautiful. And ready to open." She hated thinking about the loving care that had been brought to that space only to be destroyed.

"They broke all the tables and chairs and spray painted the walls with some really ugly graffiti." Amanda set the coffeepot down and placed both hands protectively on her rounded belly. "They even went in and destroyed Kiley's office. Ruined her computer, broke the printer. It's just a mess. The whole place."

"But who would've done such a terrible thing?"

Amanda looked around the diner, her gaze flicking across all of the familiar faces there before coming back to meet Mia's eyes. "To tell you the truth, I don't have a clue."

Mia winced. "Beau Hacket?"

Amanda nodded. "I'm sure he and his friends, like the Gordon brothers or Paul Windsor, are right at the top of the list. I know lots of people in town were against this, but I just can't picture someone I've known my whole life being so vicious."

"They'll still open the day care though, won't they?" Mia asked, hating to think that the wonderful place would never welcome children.

"You bet they will," Amanda told her. "Those of us who support the center are going to make sure of it." She took a breath and said, "Anyway, how're you doing this morning?"

"Not good," Mia admitted.

"Yeah. I, um, noticed you're not wearing your ring...."

She looked at her own naked finger, then dropped her left hand into her lap. "No, I gave it back to Dave last night."

"Aw, sweetie, I'm sorry."

"Thanks," Mia said with a tight grimace she hoped would pass as a smile. "Me, too."

"You need sugar. Cinnamon roll. On the house."

Mia didn't think she could eat anything, since for the first time in forever, food held no appeal. But she appreciated the gesture. "Thanks, Amanda."

Her friend patted Mia's hand and gave her a supportive smile. "It'll get better, sweetie."

"It has to," Mia said. Because she was so far down, there was nowhere to go but up.

The next couple of days were hard.

Dave worked himself into exhaustion all day and then lay awake all night. He couldn't stop his brain from racing. Couldn't stop the leapfrogging of thought to thought to thought.

There was Alex Santiago—still missing and no one had a clue where to look for him next. There was the destruction of the day-care center at the TCC. As far as he knew, there were no clues to the perpetrators there, either. He hadn't had a chance to talk to Nathan, so he knew nothing more than what was reported in the local paper, and judging by that, there were no suspects yet.

Then there was TexCat—and the deal for his beef that was at the heart of everything that had happened over the past month. He'd gotten that deal and had lost Mia. He'd secured his ranch's future—his organic beef would now have the stamp of excellence recognized all over Texas. With that contract in hand, he could grow his herd and expand his contacts. It was all good. But his personal future looked pretty damn grim.

His room still smelled of her. Her scent clung to her pillow, and when he reached across the cool sheets in the middle of the night blindly searching for her, he came up empty.

Hell, he couldn't even take a shower anymore without remembering the two of them on that wide bench seat. How Mia had looked with water streaming down her beautiful body. How she'd clutched at him and called his name. How she'd made him feel…whole.

Delores made his favorite foods, hoping to cheer him up, but how the hell could he choke down that mocha fudge cake when all he could think about was how much Mia had loved it?

Mike worked the ranch alongside Dave, but the foreman was so damn happy with Dave's mother he was hard to be around. And as for Alice Firestone, the woman was bound and determined to make sure that her son knew he was the instigator of his own misery.

"You've been many things in your lifetime, David," she said now over a glass of wine. "But I've never known you to be a coward."

His head snapped up and he looked at her through narrowed eyes. He was too tired for this. Tired down to his bones. He'd spent the day on his horse, riding over the acreage that meant so much to him. Losing himself in the land because that was all he had left. Now it was night again and he wasn't looking forward to trying to sleep in that big, empty bed upstairs.

She waved away his furious look. "Don't think you worry me with that lord-of-the-range glare. You can't fool me. I know you're hurting."

"You're wrong," he said flatly, and tossed his glass of sixty-year-old scotch down his throat as if it were foul-tasting medicine. The burn through his system was the only warmth he'd felt in days.

He wondered idly where the hell Mike was. Once the foreman arrived, they could sit down to dinner and this interrogation of his mother's would end.

"I'm not wrong, and that's what's bothering you," she said. Like a pit bull with a bone, his mother never let go once she'd clamped onto something. "You and I both know you miss Mia."

He poured more scotch. "I never said I didn't."

"Never said you did, either, but we'll let that go for the moment." Alice took a sip of her wine, set the glass down on a side table and crossed the wide great room to her son's side.

Heat from the fire in the hearth reached out to them and the crackle and hiss as flames devoured wood were the only sounds for a moment or two. Dave poured himself another drink, thinking he was going to need it.

Alice had been at him for two days, demanding that he do the right thing for himself—and for Mia. But he'd tried to do the right thing and

Mia had shot him down. He'd offered her marriage and had that offer tossed back into his face.

Of course, his mind taunted him, you didn't offer her what she *needed* to hear….

Scowling down at his scotch, he tossed that one back, too. But when he reached for the bottle to pour another, his mother's hand on his arm stopped him. "David, that's not the answer."

"Not looking for an answer, Mom."

"You should be," she told him. "But since you won't, I'll just give it to you."

He groaned and shook his head. "Could you just leave this alone, Mom?"

"No."

"Didn't think so."

"Your problem is, you love Mia and you're afraid to admit it."

"I'm not afraid," he said tightly, though a part of him wondered if she wasn't right.

"Of course you are," she told him, taking one of his hands into hers and squeezing it. "When your father left us, you closed in on yourself."

He frowned. Yeah, he knew that, but for some reason, he'd always thought he'd been successful at hiding it from his mom. He should have known better.

"I saw it happening, but I didn't know how to fix it," she said softly.

He didn't want her feeling guilty about any of this. She'd done her best by him when his own damn father hadn't cared enough to stick it out and try. "Mom—"

"No, listen to me, David." She turned her face up to his and met his gaze squarely. "You were protecting yourself. A little boy who was so hurt he didn't know what to do with himself. But, David, you can't stay locked away your whole life."

"I'm not," he insisted, though his argument sounded hollow even to himself.

"Your father made mistakes. But he wasn't afraid to say the words *I love you.*"

"No," Dave said wryly. "He just was too much of a coward to stay and see to his family."

"Maybe it was cowardly, maybe it was something else. We'll never know," Alice said, her voice nearly lost in the crackle of the fire. "But if you let what he did inform the decisions you make now, don't you understand that you're cheating yourself?"

"Hey," Mike called from the doorway. "Sorry I'm late."

Alice gave her son's hand one last pat, then turned to greet her fiancé. The older man bent his head for a kiss and Dave watched as his mother threw her arms around Mike for a big hug.

He smiled to himself, grateful now that the first shock of seeing his mother with a man was over, that she'd found happiness again. That she'd found love.

And maybe she was right to call him a damn coward. Hadn't his mother suffered more than he had? Losing her husband, her home, her livelihood? She'd become a single mother overnight and Dave had never once heard her complain or even bad-mouth his father.

Instead, she'd gone on. Built a life for herself and her son. She hadn't wasted time worrying over a past that was dead and gone.

How could he do less?

"Dave?" Mike asked from across the room. "You okay?"

He looked at his foreman. "Yeah. I think I am. Or anyway," he added as his mind started clicking, "I think I will be."

The following night when the doorbell rang, Mia left the email she'd just received and went to answer it. She grabbed the bowl of Halloween candy, ready to greet yet another group of kids shouting, "Trick or treat!" With a smile she didn't feel plastered to her face, she opened the door and looked into familiar, fog-gray eyes.

"Dave? What're you doing here?" She looked past him and saw ghosts and vampires and one tiny Chewbacca running up to the house across the street. "How did you get past the gate guard? I told him not to let you in."

He frowned. "Explains why it took fifty bucks instead of twenty this time."

"Oh, for—" Of course he'd bribed the gate guard. Why wouldn't he? Dave Firestone did whatever he had to do to get what he wanted. She grabbed the edge of the door and tried to shut it, but he was too fast for her.

He slapped one hand to the heavy oak panel and said, "Let me in, Mia. Please."

Surprised that he even knew that word, she could only nod and step back.

"What do you want, Dave?"

He snatched his hat off and tossed it to the couch behind him. "That's gonna take some time."

God, he looked so good. Lamplight played over his features and pooled around the two of them as if locking them into a golden bubble of light. It had been three days since she'd seen him and it felt like forever. Mia's every instinct screamed at her to throw herself at him. To lose herself in the heat of him. To kiss him again and feel the electrical charge sizzle between them.

Heck, she'd been so lonely, there was part of her ready to tell him she'd accept his stupid contract. That she didn't need him to love her. All she needed was *him.* But if she did that, gave in to her own urges, then she would be cheating them both out of what they could have had.

"Trick or treat!"

Mia jolted and clutched the bowl of candy to her chest. "I'm sorry. Kids."

She forced herself to smile as she turned to the ballerina and the soldier standing on her front porch.

"Don't you guys look great?" she said, holding the bowl out to them. She felt Dave standing right behind her and it made her so nervous she had to grip the bowl to keep from dropping it. "Take two each."

"Thank you!" they answered, then ran off the porch and down the steps to their parents, who were waiting on the sidewalk.

Mia waved the family off, fought down the pang of realization that she would never have children with the man she loved then closed the door and turned to face the man who held her heart even though she couldn't have him. Steeling herself against whatever might be coming, she said, "Okay, Dave, what is it?"

"I want you to marry me."

"I can't believe you came all the way over here to offer me the same empty proposal." Regret and disappointment twisted together in the pit of her stomach. She shook her head and said, "I'm not interested in a contract, Dave. I already told you that."

"I didn't say anything about a contract."

Then what did he mean? And why was he here? That blasted bit of hope that was still lying buried in the bottom of her heart began to warm. Mia looked up at him and waited.

Dave stared into her deep blue eyes and started talking. Words rushed from him in a torrent. Didn't seem to matter that he'd been practicing a perfectly good speech all the way over here. Because it was gone and all he was left with was what was in his heart. He hoped to hell it would be enough.

"Mia, these past few days without you…" He scraped both hands through his hair, then let them drop to his sides again. "I know now what it feels like to walk around with a gaping hole in your chest where your heart used to be."

He reached for her, but she stepped back and he couldn't blame her. He hadn't given her a reason yet to come *to* him. But he was finally ready.

Talking to his mother had helped. But the bottom line was that over the past few empty, lonely days, he'd finally realized that life without Mia wasn't worth living. He loved her. Whether he admitted it or not, he loved her. So why shouldn't she know it?

Reaching into his shirt pocket, he pulled out a ring box.

She shook her head and said, "I'm not taking that ring back, Dave."

"And I wouldn't expect you to." He grimaced tightly. "That other ring was big and gaudy and bought for all the wrong reasons. I was making a statement. Showing off. For this proposal, for the *real* proposal, I needed a ring that meant something." He opened the jeweler's box and showed her the new ring he'd purchased just that afternoon.

It was smaller than the other one. Three carats instead of five. The setting was different, too. No more modern, coldly elegant cut. This ring reminded him of Mia. Warm. Traditional. Steady.

She gasped when she looked at it and one hand

crept up to the base of her throat as she lifted her gaze to his. "It's beautiful."

"The minute I saw it, I knew it was yours."

"Dave—"

"Do you remember," he asked, cutting her off neatly, "when I gave you that other ring, I said that it would tell everyone that Mia belongs to Dave?"

She chewed at her bottom lip, swiped at a stray tear trailing from her eye and nodded, clearly unable to speak.

"Well, this one's different," he told her quietly. "This one says Dave's heart belongs to Mia."

Her hand covered her mouth now and tears were streaming down her cheeks. Every tear tore at him and Dave made a mental vow to never make her cry again.

"I don't know what to say." Her voice was choked, raw with emotion.

"Nothing yet," he said, stepping in closer, pleased when she didn't move back and away from him. "I'm not near finished talking."

She snorted a short laugh. "Always in charge..."

He gave her a half smile. “Always. Well, until tonight.”

“Trick or treat!”

Dave laughed. Most important moment of his life being interrupted by groups of kids out for candy.

“Oh, God, I can’t answer the door crying, I’ll scare the kids.” She swiped at her face, but Dave just picked up the candy bowl, opened the door and took care of things. When he stepped back inside, he set the bowl down and turned back to her.

“I’ve got a few more things to say and I’d like to get ’em said before the next crew of trolls and princesses shows up.”

She laughed a little and nodded. “Go ahead.”

“I’ve done some thinking and I finally realized that a contract is just as easy for some people to break as a promise is.” He frowned to himself and took a breath before saying, “I was so busy getting everything on the dotted line, it didn’t occur to me that if someone wants to lie or cheat…or leave, a contract won’t stop ’em.”

“No, it wouldn’t,” Mia whispered.

"But a promise made by someone who keeps their promises is as good as gold, right?"

She nodded. "Absolutely."

"Well, I keep my promises. And I want to make you one right now, Mia," Dave said, choosing every word carefully now because the next few minutes would decide his future and he for damn sure wanted to get it right. "I promise that I will always love you—"

Mia gasped, clapped a hand to her heart and started crying again. Made a man weak in the knees to see a strong woman cry—especially if he knew he was the cause. "Don't cry anymore, Mia, you're killing me."

"Dave..."

"I'm not afraid to say it now," he told her, reaching out to wipe away her tears with a gentle swipe of his thumbs. "I always thought if I never said the words, then I wasn't risking anything. But by not saying them, I was losing everything." He smiled at her. "And you know I don't like to lose."

"I know."

"So I'm promising you a lifetime of being loved. I want to marry you, Mia. I want our kids to wear that christening gown my mom gave you," he said, then paused and winced. "But not the boys, okay?"

She laughed and nodded. "Okay. We'll find manly outfits for our sons."

He grinned. "That's a deal. *Our sons and daughters.* Sounds good, doesn't it?"

"It sounds wonderful, Dave," she said, stepping up close to him. "It sounds perfect."

"Then marry me, Mia. Wear my ring. Tell the whole world that you hold my heart."

"Oh, Dave, of course I'll marry you." She watched as he plucked the ring from its velvet liner and slid it on her finger. He kissed it as if to seal it into place, then looked into her eyes.

"And you'll come home with me."

"As soon as I'm out of candy."

He grinned. "Tell me you love me."

"I love you so much," she said.

"Promise me forever," Dave whispered.

"I promise I will love you forever, Dave Firestone," she said, her heart in her eyes.

"That's all I'll ever need." He kissed her then, sealing their promises to each other.

As her arms came around him and he pulled her in close, Dave felt his world come back into balance. With Mia, with love, he had the world.

Then the doorbell rang and laughing, they handed out candy together.

* * * * *